The Collected Stories of

Carol Wobig

Carol Wobig

HIDDEN TIMBER BOOKS
MEANINGFUL BOOKS AND STORIES

MILWAUKEE, WISCONSIN

Hidden Timber Books LLC
5464 N Port Washington Rd #C224
Milwaukee, WI 53217
www.hiddentimberbooks.com

Publisher's Note: This is a work of fiction. Names, characters, places, and incidents are a product of the author's imagination. Locales and public names are sometimes used for atmospheric purposes. Any resemblance to actual people, living or dead, or to businesses, companies, events, institutions, or locales is completely coincidental.

Book Layout ©2015 BookDesignTemplates.com

The Collected Stories of Carol Wobig / Carol Wobig   1st ed.
ISBN 978-0-9906530-7-3 (paperback)
        978-0-9906530-6-6 (hard cover)

Contents

Acknowledgements

With tears in my eyes at the thought of all who have helped me write these stories, I thank, first, Judy Bridges, founder of Redbird Studio, and Kim Suhr, who carried on the writing community with Red Oak Writing. Thanks also to all my roundtable leaders and writers for their valuable input over the years.

Thanks to my publisher, Lisa Rivero, and my editor, Christi Craig, for putting it all together.

And thanks to my brother and sister-in-law for asking 'How's the book coming along?' every week at our Friday night suppers.

For Judy Bridges

1   THE PIANO

They'd had their differences, Marge and Bud, a lot of differences, but he'd always done what she'd asked of him, except let her die first. He fell over shoveling snow. What nerve. It happens a lot, but still, he should have known better. Don't shovel snow when you're seventy-one. But that's over, he's in the ground, and Marge is ready to join him. She just needs a decent burial dress, one she will make herself. No ruffles. Her daughter would choose a dress with ruffles. She was sure of that.

Bathed in a thin film of sweat from dragging a ladder up from the basement, and glad she hadn't had a heart attack in her oldest housedress, Marge sat down at the table and had a cup of coffee and two donuts—hers and one intended for Bud—and wrote the daily postcard she sent to her sister.

Sun. a.m.

Dear Irene,

Went to early mass. I'm sewing my funeral dress today. Will you be able to get along without me?

Marge

She opened the ladder next to the window in the dining room, stood on the second rung, brushed off the thin line of dust that topped each pleat of the drapes, and then removed them from the rods. She laid them on the dining room table and ripped the stitches out of the pleats. That was a job. She trimmed away the good material. It was faded but there was enough to make herself a dress with a gored skirt, an out-of-date style, but most of it wouldn't show. She found an old pattern in her sewing basket, saw herself laid out in the dress, her pearls resting on her chest, a rosary entwined in her waxy fingers. Yes. That would all do.

Now, all she really had to worry about was how to end it all. She didn't want to damage her face: she did want to look good in the casket. Pills maybe? She had a stash of Bud's in the nightstand. And she had to do it without anyone knowing it was her choice. The Catholic Church didn't look kindly on suicide. It sent you straight to hell, and you couldn't have a Mass and be buried in the cemetery.

THE NEXT MORNING—she'd stayed up until midnight sewing—her neck ached, her shoulders, her wrists. Before she got back to work, she opened the front door to check the weather, her arthritic fingers wrapped around a hot cup of coffee. Snowflakes edged the branches of the trees and drifted down on the still-green lawn, all the more beautiful because soon she wouldn't have to worry about getting the sidewalk shoveled, wouldn't have to worry about anything. By lunchtime, the skirt was complete. After a peanut butter sandwich and a piece of blueberry pie, a la mode, she went to the front door to check the sidewalk, and across the street on the strip of grass next to the curb, saw, what—a piano? Yes, a piano, a battered upright, angled toward the street, the black keys lined with a fine layer of snow. How foolish.

Mon. noon

Irene,

Too bad your mind has abandoned you. There is a piano out in the snow. You played so beautifully. I wish you were here, not out at the home.

Marge

She clothes-pinned the postcard onto the mailbox and went back to work on the dress. She made a simple top on her mother's old Singer—a collarless vee-shaped bodice with raglan sleeves. The up and down motion of the treadle, the efficiency of the needle traveling along the edge of the material, were a comfort. She'd never been close to her mother, always wanted her approval, but never quite managed that, never managed anyone's really, not even her own. Somewhere out there was a child she had abandoned, had been forced to abandon when she was fifteen. The guilt remained.

She was ready to attach the bodice to the skirt but needed a break. At the front door, she massaged her tight neck. The piano was still there. A yellow piece of construction paper wilting in the snow, was taped to the side and said FREE in big black lettering. Marge had always wanted to play the piano. But it was too late. She had other plans.

After supper, the dress was complete. Before she got into her nightgown, she gave it a try. A pin she'd forgotten scraped the soft flesh of her underarm and brought tears to her eyes. She sat on the edge of the bed and pulled herself together before she looked in the mirror. Bud would have approved, but that didn't matter. Soon she would be next to him in the cemetery.

IN THE MORNING, before she went down to the kitchen, she looked out the upstairs window. The piano. Still there. The piano, the piano. Stop. She had more important things to think about.

As she fried herself an egg, her daughter yoo-hooed from the back door. Melody never knocked.

"I was going to shovel your sidewalk, but I see it's done."

"The neighbors. Sit down, and I'll make you some breakfast."

"Thanks. Just an egg. No toast. What's with that piano across the street?'

"It's been there since yesterday. It's free. There's a sign on it."

"I think I'll give it a try when I leave. I might take it," Melody said.

Marge nodded. She didn't want it, did she? No, she didn't want a piano. Melody could have it.

After breakfast, her daughter walked across the street, brushed the snow off the keys and played a few chords. In second grade, Melody had taken lessons for a month or two at Marge's urging. She'd practiced at the neighbors. When she dropped the lessons, the first ending of her life of beginnings and endings, Bud felt he'd been right in not investing in a piano.

When her daughter's car was out of sight, Marge put on her boots and coat and walked across the street. She wanted to touch the keys. They were cold, like the ones she'd been allowed to touch only under her mother's supervision. Her dad slept during the day and came roaring out of the bedroom, belt in hand, if she or her brothers woke him up. Their sister Irene was the exception, his favorite. She could practice at any time and not cause an explosion.

"Could I take lessons, too?" Marge asked one night as she did her math homework at the kitchen table while Irene practiced and her mother made supper.

"Oh, honey," her mother said without turning around from the pot she was stirring on the stove. "I wish you could. But there's only money for one of you, and Mrs. Wright says that Irene has the talent."

But this morning, standing in the snow, Marge was alone. Her dad wasn't sleeping, her mother wasn't watching. Marge pushed one key down. Another. And another. They sounded fine to her, even though she didn't have any talent. And a lot of good that talent did Irene, now. She sat out at the home, lost. So lost.

The front door of the house behind the piano opened and Marge drew her hand back from the keys like she'd touched a hot burner. A young woman in a sweatshirt, jeans, and slippers came down the shoveled walk and stood next to her. She carried a blue tarp. "You can have that," she said. "The people we bought the house from left it behind. Neither of us can play." She smiled and patted her belly. "We need the room for the baby." She extended her hand to Marge. "I'm Tina."

"Nice to meet you," Marge said and shook Tina's

warm hand. "Why did you put the piano out in the snow?"

"We weren't paying attention to the weather report. We wanted to get it out of the way so we could paint."

"Pink or blue?" Marge smiled at Tina and then brushed the snow off the tray that was meant to hold the music.

"Green. We're waiting to see what we're having."

"That's good, how it was in the old days." She rested her finger on Middle C, the only key she could identify.

"Would you like the piano? Maybe your kids could move it for you."

"No — or I'm not sure. I'd have to hire movers. My son is in California. And my daughter might want it. Could I think about it for an hour or two?"

"Sure. Sure. Let's get it covered."

Together, after dusting off the snow, they draped the tarp over the piano, tucked it into the panel over the keys. The FREE sign remained.

"Thanks," Tina said. "I'm freezing. Talk to you later."

"Okay."

"Marge," Tina called from her front door. "I'll get my husband and his friends to move it for you if you want it."

Marge turned, waved. A lightness rose in her chest she hadn't felt for a long time, but she squelched it as she focused on getting into her house without falling on the ice.

The dress lay on the ironing board in the light of the dining room windows, ready to be pressed for the last time. She turned on the iron, sat down for a cup of coffee. What would she do with a piano? Bud would think she was crazy. She was crazy; she didn't want to be waylaid by a piano.

Steam rose from the iron. She pressed each gore, first on the inside, then on the outside. She did have a talent for ironing. Mother had told her that over and over. And this was her funeral dress. She pressed the bodice, smoothed the right raglan sleeve, looked up. Against the windows would be a good place for a piano. Even without the drapes that hadn't been open in years, the windows were safe from the neighbor's eyes, screened by the tall branches of the bushes. A private place to practice. Practice? Again she extinguished the lightness in her chest. She laid the perfectly ironed dress over her arm, carried it up the stairs, zipped it into a plastic garment bag, and hung it in the closet.

THE NEXT DAY WAS TUESDAY, her day to visit Irene. Could Marge carry out her plan and abandon Irene? Would it matter?

Meadowview wasn't a bad place, just so depressing: men and women, some of them younger than she was, trapped in all stages of decline. She walked down the hall to Irene's room—it didn't smell bad today—and listened for her sister's ranting.

Silence.

Marge relaxed. Irene was asleep in the recliner, her head leaning toward her shoulder. Marge wiped a string of drool from her sister's chin, filled her cookie box with Oreos, sat down and watched her breathe. Her ribs barely moved, and Marge once again prayed to her mother. Please take her. She was your favorite. Please take her. Irene was so alone. Marge was the only one who visited her.

"Who are you?" Irene asked when she woke up.

"Marge. Your sister. The one who sends you a postcard every day." Several of them were scattered across Irene's end table amidst used tissues, empty pill cups, and a half-eaten apple. Marge straightened up the mess.

"I don't have a sister and I need to pee."

"Okay." Marge pushed the call bell and when Nurse Ellen answered, squeezed Irene's hand, and left. Most days she only stayed for an hour, that was as much as she could bear, but could she abandon her completely?

By the time she got home, she knew she couldn't. She'd have to postpone her own death plans until Irene died. Before she took her coat off, she looked out the front door. It was still there. She rang Tina's doorbell.

"I'll take the piano," Marge said, "if your husband and his friends can move it."

"Great," Tina said. "I'll put a sold sign on it."

"Thanks," Marge said. "Thanks." During the afternoon, she kept looking out the front window. FREE was crossed out, was replaced with SOLD. Sold. What had she been thinking, that she, Marge, could learn to play the piano? She should join Irene at the home. Before supper, just before the scheduled move, she put on her coat and boots, walked as far as the curb, took a deep breath of the cold air, and walked back into the house.

Tina's men, with much grunting and laughing, maneuvered the piano across the street, up the front steps, through the front door, and into the dining room.

"That's a beautiful table," Tina's husband said as they pushed the piano into place against the windows.

"We never used it much," Marge said." We ate in the kitchen." Bud's mother had given it to them when they got married and inspected it for scratches at every holiday dinner. "How about a trade?" Marge said. "There's not really room for it with the piano. And it needs to be refinished. It's yours."

"Well, okay," Tina's husband said. "If you change your mind, let Tina know. We'll bring it back."

Marge nodded. She wouldn't miss the table. After they took it apart and carried it across the street, Marge rolled up the faded rug that had been underneath it for years and slid it down the basement stairs. Bud must be rolling in his grave, but she didn't care. And Melody. She could buy her own piano.

During the night, on her third trip to the bathroom, she made her way down the stairs to check on the piano. A full moon cast a slant of light through the bushes, through the windows, onto one end of the piano, and onto the floor that needed to be polished. She dragged her fingers across the keys, but didn't press them down.

Weds. a.m.

Irene,

I've lost my mind. Have the piano in the dining room. Am looking through the Want Ads for a teacher.

M.

CAROL WOBIG

2 THE INSTITUTE

Once again I was the new kid in school. I sat alone on the last seat of the bus and admired Mrs. Johnson's blond hair. Was twelve old enough to dye my hair? I wasn't sure. She stopped and dropped me off next to our mailbox. I jumped down to the road.

"See you in the morning, Alice," she said and swished the doors shut.

After the back of the bus disappeared around the curve beyond the next farm, I checked for mail. None, as usual. I sniffed the air, hoped to catch a whiff of something cooking in the oven of the old farmhouse that was our new home. Only the damp smell of the thin layer of snow on the ground came to me. Oh well, I would make supper.

On the way up the hill, I sang "Goin' to the Chapel, and we're gonna get mar-ar-ar-ried — " I loved that song, and even though I knew I shouldn't, I cracked the thin skin of ice just forming on the puddles in the ruts of the driveway with the toes of my new saddle shoes.

At the top of the hill, I stopped. A long black car with square fenders was parked under the oak tree next to the porch. Company? We didn't get company. But why were the greasy kitchen windows lit up as if there was a party going on?

I walked down the hill and read the lettering on the door of the car—Wisconsin Institute for the Mentally Insane. The top half of the "I" of Insane hung in a limp loop against the car door. I reached out to smooth it back in place, but stopped myself, and headed toward the barn to feed the cats. The spring on the screen door twanged.

"Alice," my dad yelled out into the yard.

I didn't move.

"Alice!"

The thump of his heavy work boots on the hollow porch shook loose my voice. "Over here, Dad." I walked toward him.

"Come inside," he said.

In the too-bright kitchen, a woman sat at the table, a navy blue coat draped over her shoulders. She wore a silky white blouse, and her hands rested on a tan folder. She smiled up at me. Dad moved back into the doorway.

"I'm going out to start the chores," he said and walked out the door.

"Sit down, Alice," the woman said, as if it was her house.

I sat down. While the woman's words came at me — *depression, suicide, doctors, hospital*—I concentrated on the pearly, rose-shaped buttons nestled in the placket of her blouse. Tiny green leaves on either side of the flowers held the buttons in place.

My mother had tried to kill herself. She swallowed all of her pills, wandered out to the highway, and collapsed in the ditch. I pictured her lying by the road, a large mound in the snow wrapped in a flowered apron. Were her thighs exposed, or worse, her underwear? A neighbor driving into town saw her, stopped and ran up to the house and called an ambulance.

I interrupted the words still coming at me. "I'll stay home," I said, "and take care of her. I can cook. I make supper most nights. I'll watch her every minute." The buttons wobbled and blurred.

The woman offered me a handkerchief, an ironed and neatly folded square of cotton edged with pink crocheting.

I hesitated.

"You can keep it," she said, smiling, and slid her handkerchief across the table.

I picked it up and blew my nose. The soft material smelled sweet.

"You need to go to school," she said and stood up. She slipped her arms into the satiny sleeves of her coat and picked up the folder. "Tell your dad I'll call him tomorrow."

I nodded and sat at the table and picked at the cracks in the oilcloth until I could no longer hear her car. I brought the damp wad of hanky up to my nose again, smelled the perfume, got up and made supper.

When I heard Dad outside the door, scraping the manure off the soles of his boots, I set the grilled cheese sandwiches on the table, the bread browned to just the darkness he liked. "When's Mom coming home?" I asked, before he got lost in reading one of his tattered magazines from the Goodwill store.

"I don't think she'll be coming home," he said and opened the *National Geographic* that sat next to his plate.

I knew not to push him too far, but I would get my mother back.

DURING RECESS the next day, I sat on the last swing, waiting.

Finally, Mrs. Williams, holding the handle of the end-of-recess bell, appeared on the top step. The pleats of her red skirt traveled over her belly and ended at her ankles. I promised myself I would never wear a skirt like that. She looked out at the kids, at her watch, back at the kids, back at her watch. Rang the bell. The playground noises descended to the shuffle of the kids' shoes on the pebbly blacktop. I dawdled as they lined up to go in for afternoon classes, made sure I was last in line.

When I reached the corner of the building, I checked for any lurking teachers, and then ran as fast as I could past the building, through the thicket of trees behind the school and out to Hwy. G, the road to The Institute. I arranged the collar of my coat up around my face and walked north on the gravel shoulder. Cars and trucks flew by until a clunker slowed down and pulled over. It backed toward me and a black-haired man hung his head out the window and yelled back, "Need a ride?"

Inside the car, the warm air of the heater blew on my cold feet that rested on receipts and beer cans and greasy red mechanic's rags. A hundred cigarette butts were crumpled in the ashtray.

"Where ya goin'?" he asked.

"To see my mother. She's in the hospital."

"Ain't no hospital out this way," he said, swiveling his head between me and the road. The right lens of his glasses was cracked and smeared with fingerprints.

"The Institute."

"That ain't a hospital," he said. "It's a nuthouse."

"It's a hospital," I said and gripped the edge of the seat with both hands as he passed an old pickup truck. Nuts and bolts rolled back and forth across the dashboard. He blew a stream of smoke against the yellowed windshield.

"What's yer name, little Miss Know-It-All?"

"Alice."

"Mine's Razor." He grinned at me and ran a dirty fingernail up the scar that ran through his whiskers. "Pleased to meet ya." He thrust his hand toward me.

I looked out the window. *Razor, the man's name is Razor.* We were moving too fast for me to jump out.

He moved his hand closer to my breast. "Didn't yer crazy ma teach you no manners? Shake my hand."

I touched the tips of my fingers to his greasy ones. "Are we close to the hospital?" I asked and moved closer to the door.

"Yup, we're almost there," he said and flipped his cigarette out the window. "But first, we're gonna stop here." He turned onto a dirt road marked Amvets Park. "Yes indeedy. First we're gonna stop here." He drove farther into the park and pulled into a clearing that had two picnic tables and an outhouse.

I reached for the door handle.

"Don't do that," he said.

I dropped my hand back into my lap.

He stopped the car and slid toward me.

"Now yer gonna kiss me," he said and reached up and grabbed a handful of my hair.

My scalp burned. His sharp whiskers ripped into my skin.

"You bitch," he said. "Open yer mouth."

His smoky, beery tongue jammed itself through my lips, past my teeth and into my mouth.

He crawled up on top of me, panted and pushed, and knocked my head against the window. When he grabbed my crotch, I stretched my jaws as wide as I could and bit down with all my strength on the livery blob of flesh flailing around in my mouth. He reared back and hit his head on the windshield.

"You bitch!"

I opened the door. We both flew out onto the ground. I was up and running.

"You bitch!"

I looked back. He was on his knees, gasping for breath. I kept running, out of the park, across the highway, through a ditch and into a cornfield. Ran until the pain in my side stopped me. In the shelter of the cornstalks, I listened, didn't move until I heard an angry squeal of tires on the blacktop.

I wanted to sit down in the muddy furrow and cry, but didn't want to get my skirt dirty before I got to The Institute, so I stood and cried into my crusty handkerchief. An incoming flock of geese honked and circled above me.

"Leave me alone," I yelled up at them. I cleaned up

my snotty face and followed a row of brittle cornstalks back to the highway.

Around the next curve, The Institute loomed—bars on the windows—no humans in sight. I walked up the circular driveway. Stopped and wiped the mud off my shoes with a handful of damp leaves.

ENTER said a sign thumbtacked to the right door. Inside, a radiator hissed. I warmed my hands before I went up the four steps to the next set of double doors.

RING BELL the second sign ordered. I obeyed. Startled by the loud buzzer, I took a step back and waited.

"What do you want?" someone shouted through the closed door.

"I need to see my mother," I shouted back.

"Visiting hours are on Sunday."

"Please, I skipped school to get here. Please, I have to see her."

Keys rattled. The heavy bolt between the large doors slid back with a thud.

"Follow me." A man in a white uniform held the door open and locked it behind me. He hooked the heavy ring of keys onto his belt loop, and led me to a row of battered leather chairs lined up against the wall before yet another set of doors.

"What's your name?"

"Alice Miller."

"Wait here."

I sat on the chair closest to the doors and smoothed my hair. In the distance, I heard the tapping of typewriter keys, then footsteps coming closer and closer. The door opened. The woman from yesterday appeared.

"Alice," she said and sat in the chair next to me.

I could smell her perfume, breathed it in while the woman's words attacked me again: I couldn't see my mother today; I should not be skipping school; I could come back with Dad on Sunday. I caught the tip of my tongue between my teeth, bit down, and forced the threatening tears to go away.

On the ride home, in the car with the white lettering, I rested my head against the cold side window. I heard the woman say that her name was Mrs. Davis, but the rest of what she said piled up around me like the snow piling up on the hillsides.

After she dropped me off, I watched the taillights of her car rise and fall with the ruts in the driveway. When they disappeared into the darkness over the hill, I walked to my mother's bedroom, the creaks of the floor beneath my footsteps the only sound in the house. I sat on the edge of the bare mattress and hugged her stained pillow to myself and rocked. Rocked as all of my life I'd watched my mother rock, until I saw myself in the cracked mirror on the dresser. I stopped. Dropped the pillow back onto the bed.

In the kitchen, I rinsed out Mrs. Davis's handkerchief in the inch of cold water still in the bottom of the dishpan, hung it over the wooden towel bar next to the sink, and pulled the crocheted edges taut. I would get my mother back, that I knew, and I would have a dozen handkerchiefs, and a silky white blouse with buttons shaped like roses, and a navy blue coat. I would have that, too.

3   What Choice Do We Have

Nestled together at the east end of the convent were the priests' quarters: sanctuaries of polished wood, sparkling glass, and privilege. Starched white tablecloths, changed daily, were laundered and ironed by nuns who ate on bare tables in the refectory in the basement. As children, they had chosen this life of austerity and silence; now, in 1965, many were old women faced with changes beyond their imagining, changes decreed by the pope. Sister Beatrix double-checked the dining room table and tried to ignore the pounding in her head. She nudged a dinner plate into line, picked up a knife, and polished it with a soft cloth until a water spot disappeared. Then she polished the wedding band on her left hand, careful of its underside where the gold was worn to the thinness of paper. She'd been a Bride of Christ for thirty-seven years.

Father Mueller, stout, red-faced, balding, entered the room first. His young assistants followed. "I just don't like it," he said, before the three men stood behind their chairs and mumbled grace.

"The pope's the boss," Father Pat said as they sat down. He was Irish, handsome, the one the novices fell in love with. His black curls, blue eyes, and sweet smile were often whispered about during recreation time. "We'll have to get somebody in here to turn the altar around."

"But to say the Mass in English." Father Mueller shook his head, causing the drape of flesh beneath his chin to sway above his Roman collar. "I don't know if I can do that. It'll seem like a sacrilege."

"We'll get used to it," Father Raymond said. The plain one, he lacked hair and a chin but was kind. Was the one you hoped would be in the confession box on Saturday. "Besides, what choice do we have?"

What choice do we have? Sister Beatrix lowered the windows to a crack to keep out the street noises and smells before she served the priests deep-fried perch, mashed potatoes, coleslaw—a Lenten meal that in the past had made her mouth water but today brought bile to her throat. While change roared through the Church, a battle between obedience and disobedience raged within Beatrix.

Father Mueller buttered the mound of potatoes on

his plate. "I want to go to Rome and shake some sense into that stumpy little man."

"Better not let the archbishop hear you refer to Pope John as stumpy," Father Pat said, laughing. He spread a layer of tartar sauce over his fish.

"He won't hear about it unless you tell on me."

"Relax," Father Raymond said. "It'll all work out."

The bantering continued. Beatrix went into the kitchen and spooned dessert, cherry cobbler, into shallow bowls. Dessert in Lent. She should have been a priest. She didn't get out the ice cream that she knew was in the freezer.

"Is there any ice cream today?" Father Mueller asked when she set his bowl in front of him.

"Oh, sorry, I forgot." Beatrix went back to the kitchen, leaned into the freezer and massaged her temples before she returned to the dining room and served the ice cream. The young men finally left for a game of basketball, but Father Mueller remained. Now what did he want. She wanted to get her work done, sit somewhere quiet with her eyes closed.

"Is there any cobbler left?"

She nodded. Couldn't get the polite 'Yes, Father' to come out of her mouth.

"I want to apologize," he said, when she set the second dessert in front of him. "I didn't mean to shock you with my words about the Holy Father." He ate the cobbler in three bites and threw the napkin from his lap onto the table. A corner landed in his coffee cup, turned brown. "What do you think of all these changes?"

Sister Beatrix set the silverware in her hand back on the table, looked toward the taut curtains covering the panels of the French doors that led to the hallway. They were in place: her protection from the prying eyes of nuns on their way to chapel. "I'm not sure," she said.

"You're afraid to say?"

Noise from the courtyard caught her attention. The sound of the basketball bouncing on the asphalt filled the room; the pounding in her head increased. "It's so easy for the young ones," she said. "I think they're excited."

"Sit down and have a cup of coffee with me."

"You know I can't do that."

"Well, tell me what you think." He leaned back, his arms folded on his chest.

"The new habit," she said. "Have you seen it?"

He shook his head.

"It's knee length. Blue. No veil."

"Right up there with saying the Mass in English?"

She nodded and was surprised by the emotion that overtook her. It had been years since she'd felt the need to hold back tears. "Mother Hilda stood up there in the last meeting and told us to let our hair grow. She used

Sister Angela as an example of how we should be."

"Angela?"

Beatrix nodded. "And they want us to be in the world again. Social workers. All I know how to do is be obedient. But that's not enough. Now they want — I don't know what — dingbats."

Father Mueller laughed. "Looks to me like we old-timers are passengers on a sinking ship, and I don't think there's any way we can save ourselves." He heaved himself out of the chair. "I better get going and find someone to turn the altar around."

She watched him walk down the long corridor, saw the droop in his shoulders as he moved in and out of the panels of light cast on the floor by the open doorways.

After she set the table for supper, she went in search of Sister Wilhemena, her best friend, though they didn't have best friends in the convent. Willie was hard at work in the laundry room. A row of white altar cloths ironed to perfection and draped over silk-covered hangers hung from a clothesline strung close to the ceiling.

"How is your back doing?" Beatrix asked. She sat on a chair across from Willie and closed her eyes.

"Not too bad. I offer it up." Willie was old, bent. Her veil sagged down to her hip on the right side. A soft dollop of flesh hung on either side of her wrinkled chin.

"I'm offering up this headache," Beatrix said and inhaled the clean smell in the room, the steam from Willie's iron. She reached back and scratched the lumps beneath her veil. "Are you letting your hair grow?"

"No, I am not," Willie said.

"No?"

"No." She fed the material she had just ironed over a hanger, drew its tails into perfect alignment. "Imelda and Rosie and I are going to talk to Mother tonight. Would you like to join us?"

Sister Angela breezed into the room. "I'll take these upstairs," she said. Beatrix was sure there wasn't a Saint Angela—their professed names were supposed to be saints' names.

"Be careful," Willie said when she saw her assistant lift five hangers off the clothesline and sling the ironed cloths over her arm.

"She's supposed to be our example?" Willie said after Angela left. "All I hear is talk about hair styles." She thumped the iron back and forth over Father Mueller's Sunday chasuble.

"He's upset," Beatrix said, gesturing at the chasuble.

"Oh, what's his problem," Willie said. "All the priests have to do is say the Mass in English. We'll still be waiting on them."

"You are riled up today."

She shook the iron at Beatrix. "You bet I am. We

gave our lives to this place and now they're changing the rules."

Beatrix folded a pile of napkins, comforted by the warmth that seeped into her thighs as she shaped them into perfect triangles. Still, her head pounded.

"Your veil looks lumpy with all that hair under it."

"I know." She reached up and scratched her head again.

"And you look pale."

"I've had this headache for days." Suddenly overwhelmed with nausea, Beatrix stood up and ran to the bathroom down the hall.

"Are you okay?" Willie asked from outside the door.

"I think so. Just lost my lunch." She sat down on the toilet seat, opened the door a crack. Willie's face appeared in the opening.

"I'll be right back. Sit still." She returned with a glass of ice water and a scissors, squeezed into the tiny bathroom, handed Beatrix the water, and closed the door. "You need a haircut," she said. "It's creating pressure on your brain." She snipped at the air above Beatrix's head.

"But Mother Hilda said — "

"She's not always right."

"Well, the pope said — "

"The pope's not always right either. Let's cut that hair." Willie kept snipping away at the air. "Join the rebellion."

Beatrix laughed, removed one pin from her veil, replaced it, closed her eyes, and saw the droop in Father Mueller's shoulders as he walked down the hall after lunch. She took a deep breath, reached up and removed all the pins from her veil, released her flattened hair.

"Okay," she said.

"Okay," Willie said and began cutting. "You're one of us."

"I guess so," Beatrix said, as her grey curls drifted onto her black habit. She brushed them away. The throbbing in her head lessened and was almost gone by the time they swept up the floor and returned to work.

4   Too Much Love

It was August in Wisconsin, hot and humid in the refectory of the Mother House. The nuns sat with bowed heads and ate bowls of oatmeal with far too much clinking of their spoons. Mother Adalbert—Addie, call me Addie, she always said when introduced—could stop the meal, remind the sisters of their manners, but she didn't want to add a reprimand to their physical discomfort. Perspiration lined their upper lips, and she knew it was dampening the heavy layers of their habits. She hoped next summer would be better.

If things went as planned, if Sister Francis's paintings sold well at the craft fair, Addie hoped to be able to install an air conditioner in at least this room of the old building. They would be able to close the windows and block out the whoosh of the early morning traffic on 10th Street. Though today it was a blessing. It drowned out the voice of the novice sitting up front on the dais reading from *The Lives of the Saints*. The book in her hands trembled, as did the edge of her white veil. Poor child. She seldom made it through a sentence without stumbling over one or more words.

After breakfast, on the way to her office, Addie jotted down three reminders to herself in the small spiral notebook always in her pocket. *Ask the sisters to clink their spoons less. Ask the Mistress of Novices to see that the reader spent more time on preparation*, and a note to herself — *work on your irritability.* It seemed to be worse with the onset of menopause. When she saw Sister Ludmilla standing outside her office, she slowed her steps and reminded herself to be patient.

Ludmilla, short and plump like Addie—and meaner, she always thought — followed Addie into her office where the members of the Ruling Council sat in front of her desk on folding chairs. The open-door policy she'd instituted sometimes backfired on her.

"Good morning, Sisters," she said and walked over to the windows, tilted the blinds forward to block the morning sun, and gave herself time to collect her thoughts. Being Mother Superior turned out to be a tougher job than she'd thought. She took over just after Pope John issued directive after directive to modernize, and she only survived it with the help of Sister Francis. Her paintings contributed to the bottom line, and she was a good listener, saved Addie many times from lashing out at the wrong person.

When she was settled at her desk, Addie noted that her superiors chose not to make eye contact with her. Sister Daniel inspected her cuticles. Sister Marian picked bits of lint off her scapular. Sister Valeria, the eldest and a former Mother Superior, fingered the rosary beads draped across her lap. If Valeria was praying, the news was bad. Was it the modern habit? It had taken months to settle on a style deemed modest by Ludmilla. Perhaps the new position of the altar in the chapel. It had been turned to face the congregation. Or maybe it was the recent consignment of Mother Hildegarde's sour-faced portrait to the closet. It had hung for years on the wall of this office, but last week Addie replaced it with a painting done by Francis, a blossoming apple tree. She looked to it now to calm herself.

"You have been an asset to the community," Ludmilla began, opening the manila folder on her lap. "But it has come to our attention—"

This again. For the third time, that simple phrase introduced the same discussion: she was being accused of favoritism, inappropriate behavior. Maybe she was too friendly with the younger nuns, but they were receptive to the changes, often welcomed them, and were more fun. She would apologize as she had in the past, and it would be over. They needed her. For the first time in years, the convent was running in the black.

"Whom have I offended this time?" she asked, using the proper English she could call up when necessary.

"Sister Francis." Ludmilla handed her three typed pages.

Francis? Addie read the papers in her shaking hand. Her heart pounded.

Sister Francis felt that Addie was pursuing her, wanted a Particular Friendship, was threatening her vocation. Addie's transgressions were documented on the last page complete with dates: daffodils in April; tulips in May; the renovation of her studio; the couch; Addie's numerous visits to chat, read, or discuss her administrative problems. Her touches. A thank you hug that lasted too long.

The Council waited. Addie's face burned. She didn't have to look up to feel their eyes drilling into her. The words she needed, words that would exonerate her, would not come. The blinds, lifted away from the window by a small breeze, clacked back into place. "I need to think." She rolled up the pages, the edges damp with the sweat of her palms. She stood up.

Sister Ludmilla stood, too. "Wait, we've made a decision."

"Yes?"

"You must seek spiritual guidance and show us that

you've changed your ways, or you'll be considered unfit for religious life."

Unfit for religious life. Not the words Addie was searching for, but words she had said to other nuns, never thinking that someday they would be applied to her. No doubt the look she had seen on those nuns' faces was on her face right now.

"For the time being, you will be relieved of your duties as Mother Superior. If you could give us your decision by the end of the day," Ludmilla continued, "we would appreciate it. And of course, you're not allowed to discuss this with anyone."

Addie left the room, her mind on the chapel but her trembling legs headed toward the basement. She grasped the cold railing and made her way down the steps. Dank air assaulted her. She felt around on the concrete blocks until she found the switch for the lower lights. Dim bulbs hanging from the rafters lit up row after row of the nuns' trunks. She collapsed onto hers and reread Francis's accusations.

What Addie had thought were gestures of friendship and thanks had been interpreted as gestures of love? The kind of love forbidden in the convent. The Council mentioned Julie, too, and Angelina. They made it sound like she had a long history of Particular Friendships. She did not. They were wrong.

She folded the damning papers into a small square,

put them in her pocket, opened her trunk, and dug around until she found the clothes she'd worn on her entrance day. The white blouse was yellowed. She could poke her fingers through the pleats of the gathered skirt, and the crinoline she'd starched with such care crumbled when she tried to smooth out the wrinkles. She dropped them back into the trunk and paced, her arms crossed over her chest against the dampness invading her habit. The large Crucifix that always hung from her neck now pressed into her breast bone. She wished she still believed in God. This might be easier. She could say it was His will. But He'd abandoned her long ago, or she Him, she wasn't sure.

And Sister Francis?

Why had she abandoned Addie?

She needed to talk to her. She snuck up the back stairway to the second floor, grateful that she didn't meet anyone on the way.

Francis was at work in her studio. She leaned toward a canvas, her right arm raised, her head cocked to the left. Diesel fumes from the bus idling on the corner outside contaminated the fresh smell of turpentine always present in the room, but it was Francis's choice for a studio.

"The light is the best," she'd said.

Addie knew nothing about light and painting, but she had the desks removed and shelves installed. She'd found the funds for tubes of paint, brushes, an easel, rolls of canvas. The couch she'd bought for herself. Maybe she shouldn't have. Ludmilla thought it an extravagance.

"Frannie?"

Sister Francis straightened up but did not turn around.

Addie walked into the room and stood between her and her painting. "Why didn't you come to me?"

"I did." Francis stepped back and, with a shaking hand, stirred a blob of red paint on her palette with the tip of her brush. "You didn't listen to me."

"When?" Addie saw the tears in Frannie's eyes, had to swallow her own.

"On Easter." Francis picked up a dab of blue paint with the tip of her brush and mixed it into the red, over and over.

"Up here?" Addie said.

"No. We were walking in the garden. I told you people were talking. You told me not to worry. You would take care of it." She looked back at her painting. "But you didn't. I had to say something."

"But this?" Addie pulled the accusations out of her pocket. "You had to do this?" Her voice wobbled. "They told me I was unfit for religious life."

"You are." Francis set her palette and brush too close to the edge of the counter. They fell and sent a splash of color across the old floorboards.

Addie stepped back.

"What are you saying?"

"Can't you see it? Everyone else does."

"Everyone else does?" Addie shrank into the depths of her habit, made it over to the couch and collapsed onto it.

"It's a common topic of conversation." Francis knelt down on the floor to clean up the mess. "What a competent Mother Superior you are but how you fall in love with one sister after another."

Addie went to the counter, picked up a rag, lowered her creaky body to the floor and tried to help. "Fall in love? That's what they say?"

"Yes," Francis said. "Fall in love." She sat back on her heels. "I'm not in love with you." She sat back on her heels and wept. "I had to protect myself. I'm sorry."

Addie kept wiping away at the stain, succeeding only in pushing the paint deeper into the cracks of the old floor. "This will have to be sanded," she said.

"You're something." Francis blew her nose into the cleaning rag. "In danger of being kicked out and thinking about repairing the floor."

Addie stopped herself from reaching out and wiping away the red drop of paint on Francis's nose. "For the first time in my life, I don't know what to think."

The bell for morning prayers rang.

Francis stood up, walked to the window. In its

reflection, she removed the paint from her nose and adjusted her veil. "What's going to happen to you?"

"Go to chapel," Addie said. "Ludmilla will be watching you. I'll be fine."

"I don't want you to leave," Francis said and opened the door. "I was just so frightened for myself. I'm not strong like you are."

"Go to chapel," Addie said again.

Francis nodded and left.

Addie sat on the couch and watched a black ant make its way to the paint stain and investigate its edges. Another followed. Had she forgotten to call the exterminator? She pulled her notebook out of her pocket along with the papers naming her sins. No, there it was: *Call the exterminator*, followed by a check mark.

She'd never thought of love as one of her strengths, always thought of herself as competent but cold, and here she sat, accused of love, too much love.

She turned to a fresh page in her notebook. Made a new list:

> *Pack up her trunk one more time?*
> *Start a new life?*

She wasn't sure.

CAROL WOBIG

5   On My Knees

If only I hadn't been such a fool. I yanked another strand of quack grass out of the petunia bed next to Edna's Tap and sat back on my heels. My nails were chipped and dirty, and I massaged my aching fingers and the indent of the ring I'd worn for thirty years.

I'd made a vain attempt to remove the ring with soap on my last day as a nun. "We'll have to cut that off," Sister Ludmilla had said. "Wait here." I was hidden in the supply room behind what had been my office, changing from my habit into street clothes. When she came back with a tin snip, I held out my hand but drew it back when she shoved the tip of the tool beneath the ring. "Hold still," she said and grunted with the effort of cutting the ring. It didn't snap but broke with uneven edges that scraped my skin as she pulled it off my finger.

The indent would fade, but, ring or no ring, the shame of being asked—no, *told*—to leave the world I loved, would remain.

As would the quack grass. The roots invaded every inch of the flower beds.

"Are you out there?" Lucille called from the front door of the tavern.

"Over here," I said. She was paper thin, a cigarette always in her hand.

"Time for a break. The old guys will be here soon." She leaned against the side of the building and lit up. "Want one?"

"Not, yet," I said. We laughed. With her help, I hated that I needed her help, I'd found a place to live, a job, but smoking didn't appeal to me.

"You don't have to do this," she said and gestured toward the pile of weeds next to me.

"I know. I need to keep busy." I picked a handful of dried petunia blooms off the sticky stems.

"I'm the same way," she said. "How did we end up like this? Me an alkie pulling beers, you a defrocked nun. If our mothers could see us now." She crushed out her cigarette with the toe of the high-heeled boots she'd bought on one of our trips to the thrift store.

"I'm glad mine is dead," I said. "This would have broken her heart."

"Mine, too."

"But I'm glad you answered my letter." I wiped a little dust off the toe of her boot.

"Hey, what are cousins for," she said and poked me on the shoulder. "I better get back to work."

Lucille, my savior. She'd found a place for me to live, lent me money for the rent and to buy clothes at the thrift store. Took me to my job interview. All for a life I didn't want. I didn't want to be kneeling on the ground next to a tavern, sweating in the hot August sun of a Wisconsin summer. I wanted to be dead, as dead as the petunias would be in the fall.

I worked another half hour, until the first shift at the factory up the road let out and pickup after pickup crunched into the gravel parking lot. The slammed doors followed by men's and women's voices, people who might have known me when we were kids at the local Catholic school, sent me fleeing across the highway to The Pine Cone Mobile Home Park.

Inside the safety of my trailer, the third one on the right, I wiped the mud off my battered nun heels. My trunk, now a coffee table, and the shoes were all that remained of my former life. In search of a tin of black shoe polish, I lifted the lid of the trunk but dropped it, overwhelmed by the familiar smell of the convent storage room. What did the damaged heels matter? They would be my work shoes. I set them in the closet next to the white ones I'd bought at the thrift store.

They needed polishing, too, but would have to do until I got my first paycheck from teaching English at the high school, if I made it to the first day.

I sat at the kitchen table and started a list of things I needed on a scrap of paper, not in a small spiral notebook. White shoe polish, not black. I underlined it. Starred it. Couldn't think of anything else. White shoe polish. I lowered my head onto my crossed arms and let the tears drip onto the table.

That done, I made myself supper: tomato soup, toast, a glass of milk. I longed for the bite of the strong coffee served in the refectory at every meal and searched my almost-empty kitchen shelves. A jar of stale instant would do. Nothing. I leaned my forehead against the coolness of the tin cupboard doors, teared up, but didn't cry. I had to stop crying.

After supper, I sat out on the front steps in the humid night air and tried to read under the dim porch light. Thumping music, loud voices, and the squeal of tires drifted across the road. The huge OPEN sign on the roof of the tavern flashed through the branches of the trees, revealing my neighbor Ralph as he lurched up the driveway.

"Morning, Ginny," he said, his t-shirt draped over his shoulder blades as if on hooks.

"Good evening," I said.

He looked up at the sky. "Oh right, right. Good

evening, Ginny." He dropped his keys in the grass, left them there, and stumbled into his trailer.

"Ginny," I whispered into the darkness. "Ginny." I was no longer Mother Adalbert, Addie, superior of a community of two thousand women. Drunks and hordes of mosquitoes were my community now. One landed on my arm. I let it pierce my flesh, drink my blood — my contribution to the world for the day. I picked up Ralph's keys, laid them on his porch before I went in, then took a cold shower that I prayed would save me from my nightly sin.

Washed, drenched in talcum powder to combat the odor of the lumpy mattress on the pull-out couch, I lay down and ran my fingers through my damp hair. I picked up my rosary from the end table, fingered its worn beads, and tried, really tried to conjure up the God I used to pray to. But in the end I conjured up Sister Francis and had to set the rosary aside. I needed my fingers for other things.

Maybe the rumors I had denied for years were true.

IN THE MORNING, I wanted to go to confession. Though I didn't believe in God anymore, I still believed in hell. I left the trailer park in my white heels and a frumpy dress and headed downtown. Ralph's keys still lay on his porch, but it was early. I let them be.

Inside the church, I slid into the last pew. After

Mass, the priest announced that he would be back in a moment to hear confessions. Three white-haired women lined up next to the confessional. I didn't move, but I had to do this. Hell loomed. When the third woman stepped outside the velvet drapes, I got up.

"Bless me, Father, for I have sinned," I whispered into the latticed screen inside the dark cubicle and told him of the evil in my heart. "I am in love with another woman, a nun. I am guilty of impure thoughts and actions." The scent of his Juicy Fruit gum drifted through the screen.

"Are you a nun?" he asked and leaned farther into the screen.

"I am. No, I was."

In the silence that followed, I shifted my weight on the creaky kneeler. Someone in heels left the church. The heavy door whooshed shut.

"You are a fallen woman," he finally spat through the screen, "and will burn in hell forever if you don't rip this evil out of your heart."

My face flamed. "I know," I said. "I'm trying,"

"You must try harder," he said and traced the sign of the cross close to the screen and mumbled the words of forgiveness. "Your penance is a daily rosary."

I pulled aside the drape and hurried out of the church into the fresh air. *Unfit for religious life.* My superiors were right. I had failed, beyond failed. And I couldn't walk another step in my white heels. I took them off and threw them into the ditch. I wouldn't need them. I wasn't sure how, but I was not going to live that life.

LATER WHEN I RETURNED to the trailer from my afternoon job of weeding, I saw that Ralph's keys still lay on his porch. Was he ill? Did he need help?

I walked back to the tavern. Lucille was working. She would know what to do. There were only four pickups in the lot. I hesitated, then went into the bar, a place I'd never been before.

"Ginny!"

Lucille was hugging me before my eyes had adjusted to the darkness, to the air heavy with smoke, and to men's voices.

"Come over here," she said and led me to a stool at the end of the bar. "How about a beer?"

"Oh, no," I said and snuck a peek to my left. No one was looking my way.

"A Coke?"

"That would be fine," I said and told her about Ralph. That his keys had been on the porch since last night.

"Any of you guys seen Ralph?" Lucille shouted to the men at the bar.

"Haven't seen him," someone said.

"I wouldn't worry."

"Okay," I said. "I'm just so used to taking care of things. I can't stop myself."

We laughed. It felt good to laugh.

After supper, I did my usual, sat on the porch and tried to read while fighting off the mosquitoes, and, tonight, my worries about Ralph. Neither would leave me alone. I walked over to his trailer and knocked on the door.

No answer.

I knocked louder.

No answer.

I turned the knob, pushed the door open a bit. "Ralph? It's Ginny. Your neighbor. Are you okay?" I heard a faint cough but had to step back and take a breath of fresh air before I went in. Ralph lay on his couch in a pool of stench, his whiskered cheeks sunk into his toothless mouth.

"Help me, please," he whispered. "Help me."

I opened the windows, lifted his phone to call Lucille for help. It was dead. I ran a glass of water and held it to his lips. He drank the whole thing.

"More," he said. "Please."

"In a minute. Too much at once will make you sick." I squelched my urge to run out of there. "I'm going to clean you up," I said. "Close your eyes."

He obeyed. I held my breath as much as I could while

I stripped off his clothes, pulled the soiled blanket from beneath him, and threw the whole mess into the yard.

I filled a basin with warm water, found a clean rag and worked quickly — until I got to his genitals. I paused. Rinsed out the rag once, twice, three times, checked that his eyes were still closed, rinsed out the rag one more time and finished the job.

"Don't move," I said. I ran to my trailer and picked up a blanket and the talcum powder. I sprinkled it over his gaunt body, wrapped him in the clean blanket, saw his dentures lying just beneath the edge of the couch amidst dust balls and bread crumbs. "Do you want these in?" I asked.

He nodded.

I rinsed them off at the kitchen sink, touched them to his dry lips, slipped them onto his waiting gums.

"Thank you," he whispered and closed his eyes.

"I'm going to the tavern for help."

Lucille and some of the men followed me back across the road. In the trailer, she leaned into his face and said, "We're going to get you to the hospital."

He nodded.

One of the men stepped forward. "Well, Ralphie," he said and picked him up, "don't you smell sweet." He carried him out the front door, down the steps, and handed him over to two men sitting in the bed of the truck idling in the driveway. They wrapped their drinking buddy in another blanket and held him across their laps. One man tapped the window behind him with his knuckle. "Ready," he said.

The tail lights of the truck floated up and down over the ruts in the driveway, turned right onto the road, and disappeared.

While Lucille waited for me, I took a long shower, let the water run until it turned cold, until I could stop crying.

"Do you need to go to the store?" she asked and held up my shopping list when I came into the kitchen.

"I do." I sat down across from her, hesitated a moment, then raised my nightgown just above my knees and showed her my calluses. "I need to add lotion to that list."

"Yikes," she said, softly. "How did you get those?"

"The kneelers in the convent—bare wood."

"I never would have survived," she said and stood up.

"I didn't." I had to laugh.

"Why did you leave?" she asked.

"It wasn't the kneelers," I said.

Our eyes met.

"I shouldn't have asked." She pulled something out of the pocket of her jeans and handed it to me. "This is lip salve. Use it on those knees until we get to the store."

The tiny tube held the warmth of her body. "Thanks."

"I'd better get back to work," she said. "The boys will be in a panic."

I followed her out onto the porch.

She paused. "Well, whatever made you leave, you're still a good person. You probably saved Ralph's life tonight." She walked down the driveway and disappeared into the darkness.

Me. A good person. I didn't know anymore.

I sat down, opened the salve, and rubbed it into my calluses.

6 WHEEL OF FORTUNE MONOLOGUES*

CHARACTERS:

LIL. Fifties. Heavy. Wearing jeans and plaid shirt with wrap-around apron. Grey, stringy hair.

EDITH. Lil's sister, fifties. Average size. In terry robe. Hair in rollers.

BITSY. Seventies. Short. Blouse and pants. Permed hair.

RHONDA. Forties. Large woman. Sweatshirt, jeans, short hair.

SETTING: Small town in Wisconsin

ON STAGE: Suggestion of kitchen and living room. In kitchen, table for characters to sit at with cup of coffee. In living room, recliner or easy chair in front of TV. *Wheel of Fortune* tape playing throughout performance.

Each character does her monologue at a table and moves toward the living room. When stage goes dark, the next character comes in and sits at the table.

---

*"*Wheel of Fortune* Monologues" was chosen to be performed at the Village Playhouse Twenty-First Annual Original One Act Festival in 2006 (Wauwatosa, Wisconsin).

LIL

My son picks garbage for a living. Doesn't drive a city truck, no. He literally picks garbage. Goes out every day with a black plastic bag tied to a belt loop on his jeans and comes home in a few hours with his loot.

He's such a loser. I can't stand to look at him anymore. I want to kick him out. Right now he's watching *Wheel of Fortune*. I hate that show, the noise. And that stupid Vanna. He should be doing the dishes.

I still feed him. Tonight it was macaroni and cheese and Jimmy Dean's breakfast sausages. My sister Edith and I don't agree on much, but we do agree that Jimmy Dean's Sausages are the best, and that we don't like our kids much. She has a daughter, Marion.

I don't think my son is crazy, no. Just odd. Like his dad. He spent his life in the basement. Tinkering he called it. After a few years, I never went into that part of the basement. Just went down on Saturdays to do the wash. Maybe he just sat there and stared at the wall for all those years. I don't know.

I don't admit this to many people, only to Edith, but when my husband was killed in a car accident, on that bad corner, Western and 89th, I didn't cry. It was a relief — to have one less odd person roaming around this house waiting to be fed. It was a relief.

I only married him because that's what was left. I wasn't a pretty girl. Frumpy and dumpy, that was me. My mother thought I was pregnant, but I wasn't. I wouldn't let him near me down there until we were married. I hated it. Sex. All that rubbing, him pushing that thing in, me feeling like I had a tree trunk on top of me, taking the breath right out of me. Soon as I knew I was pregnant, I put an end to that pretty quick.

Being pregnant was no joy either. The morning sickness, my body, as if it wasn't big enough to start out with, grew into a Mack Truck. My big tits hung on my big belly. I had to pee all the time. And then the delivery. I don't even like to think about that. Strangers in white coats looking at me down there. If it had been up to me, I would have had a bag over my head the whole time.

And now I have this twenty-five-year-old oddball, garbage-picking son, sitting across from me, night after night, in a recliner he found in the alley. I never did like him. Right from the start. I thought I would, but I didn't. The crying, the smells, him hanging on my leg, needing me. And I like him less now. If he'd just get a job and get out of here. Come to visit on Sundays. I could handle that. Maybe I should cut off the food, keep the Jimmy Dean's for myself, though I don't know if I could go that far.

Every night I have to yell at him to stop drooling over Vanna and get out in the kitchen and do the dishes. And every night we have the same fight. He runs too much water when he does the dishes. Rinses them one by one with the water running. I've told him a hundred times, stack the dishes in the drainer, then rinse them with the hose.

Eddie, get out here and do these dishes!

[Stage dark. Sound of gun shot over TV.]

EDITH

So there I was this morning, the grieving widow standing at the back of the church next to Ray's casket. I just went through this with my sister Lil. Her son shot her. Just like that. Shot her with a gun he found in a garbage can. Because she told him how to do the dishes. Is that nuts, or what?

And now Ray's dropped dead, just like that, out shoveling snow. He always said that was a good way to go, to drop dead. I wonder if he had time to think that on his way down into the snowbank. He wouldn't buy a damn snow-blower. Said he didn't need one.

'He looks good, Edith,' everyone said. I heard that a hundred times today. He didn't look good, he looked dead. Our daughter, Marion, Princess Marion, had the undertakers wind a rosary through his fingers. He hadn't said a rosary since the nuns forced him to in grade school.

I hate to say it, but my daughter is stupid. She insisted that we have a normal funeral with the visitation, the Mass, the limo for the ride to the cemetery. Lunch in the church basement. All that show. I mean, we could have had him cremated and then bought a real nice refrigerator, the kind with the ice and water in the door.

I admit it, I've always been jealous of my daughter, but I hid it. I only call her Princess Marion in my mind, never to her face.

I probably shouldn't have married Ray. I mean, all the kids in his family were given names that start with R — Roy, Raymond, Rhonda, Rosalie and Roberta — and that should have given me a clue. But I was a fool and went ahead and married him anyway. His brother Roy, thin as a rail, was a pallbearer. He has cancer, will probably be next. Or cousin Albert. He wasn't looking great either. Seems like you get to a certain age and that's all that's out there, death.

Anyway, the Mass went on forever — readings, songs, a eulogy. The priest, who never knew Ray, went on about what a wonderful father he was. Marion must have given him that B.S. Finally it was over and we rode, just the two of us, in a big black limo to the cemetery.

After more prayers — I've said more prayers in the last month than I have for the last twenty years — we went back to the church basement for lunch. The Ladies Auxiliary, the old girls with the white hair, put it on. I admit, I was hungry.

Finally when it was over, I sent Princess Marion on her way and went home, took a roll of garbage bags upstairs, and started to empty out Ray's side of the closet. I was okay until I got to his work boots.

"You damn, fool," I yelled at the boots. I kicked them against the wall, wiped my eyes on the sleeve of one of his shirts. *Buy a damn snow-blower*, I'd told him months ago. Buy a damn snow-blower.

So I've had my cry and a shower. Now it's time for another cup of coffee and *Wheel of Fortune*. I wonder what Vanna will be wearing tonight. I do like the way she dresses.

[She gets up and walks toward living room.]

BITSY

Albert and I are short people. I haven't told this to anyone else, but I'm pretty sure that's why he married me, because I'm a little shorter than he is. He could put his arm across my shoulders when we walked home from the movies. We have stuck together for fifty-three years, and now he's dying.

We went to his cousin Ray's funeral today. Edith never shed a tear. Don't know how I'll be when the day comes for me to bury Albert. He's in watching *Wheel of Fortune*. He loves Vanna. I can't really blame him. She is pretty—and tall.

His doctors are all tall, too, and they all talk too fast. Every visit I have to ask them to repeat what they say, to spell out the medical terms. Some of them get irritated, but what am I to do. Barbara, our daughter, wants the details. She looks them all up on the computer and mails me and her brothers fat envelopes with pages full of more words that none of us understands. I've quit opening the envelopes. Everybody dies one way or another.

Albert is fading away, I can see that. His skin hangs on him like it was made for someone else. I had to buy the new shirts and pants that he wears to the clinic in the boy's department. What's more depressing is that clinic, let me tell you. People in all stages of dying. I feel sad for the ones sitting there alone. Old men mostly, their bony collarbones sticking out of the collars of their plaid shirts. Do they live alone, I wonder? Sit in front of the TV in the recliner and sleep their days away? Albert would rather I didn't talk to them, but I do.

And now during supper, he told me that he's not going to fill the bird feeders tonight, or ever again. It's been a bone of contention between us, those feeders. I've always hated the mess and the cost. We've argued about it all of our lives. The first thing he always did when we moved was hang up the darn bird feeders. Seven of them. An eighth one on order from Sears. He rigged them up on pulleys so he could reach them without using a ladder. When you're as short as we are, you have to be creative.

I've had to be creative about getting him to eat. I make little bitty meals, a scrambled egg and a half piece of toast, and serve them to him on a small plate. But I don't think I can save him. Barbara thinks I can, but I disagree. No matter what I do and no matter what chemicals they drip into him, he just gets smaller and weaker. I wake up in the night and listen for his breathing, not knowing if I want to hear him snoring or if I want to hear silence.

I asked him why he's not going to feed the birds

anymore. I thought he'd keep doing it to his dying day just to aggravate me. 'So they get used to me being gone,' he said. 'So they don't use up their energy coming here for food in the winter.'

So he's thinking of the birds, and thinking that he won't be here come winter. The birds, the birds, I'll feed the damn birds. One more cup of coffee and I'll feed the birds.

[Stage dark.]

RHONDA

Just saw my neighbor Bitsy out in her backyard in the dark, filling up Albert's birdfeeders. I wonder what came over her. She told me at Ray's funeral today that when Albert goes, the feeders go.

During the service, I noticed that the church sure could have used a good cleaning, I can tell you that. The rest room made me nervous, all that dirt waxed into the corners of the floor. I wanted to get down there with an old knife and scrape those corners clean.

Edith didn't shed a tear. She and Ray had one of those marriages that make you glad to be single. My folks did, too. Our mother was miserable, I could see that, tiptoeing around Dad, swamped with us kids. I escaped into the convent when I was fourteen, even though I wasn't religious. I just liked the nuns. Plus, I was a true goody-two-shoes, a teacher's pet. And husky—my dad's description of me. That stuck: husky.

You wouldn't think so, but even in the convent there was a group of popular girls who ran things. They were thinner and smarter and prettier, and wore the in-style of granny shoes. You remember how the nuns dressed in the old days. I wasn't in the bottom group of girls, thank God, the ones who were sent off to the kitchen for the rest of their lives. I was in the middle group, the drones. We obeyed the rules, never expressed an opinion.

The worst thing about being in the convent was the hygiene. I had acne, bad acne that you don't see much anymore, and my hair was greasy. We were allowed to shampoo only once a week, and we couldn't shave. I was a husky, hairy, greasy mess. My way to deal with it all was to daydream, and eventually I daydreamed my way right out of there.

When I left the convent, my plan was to have a wonderful life, but I ended up a ruin. I let men use me, let them drop over and drop into bed. Pathetic. I never told anyone about this, but when I was 25, I had an abortion. Me—the one of the R kids who had been in the convent had had an abortion. A lot of us R kids are oddballs. I have to admit that. I got involved with a guy who was my sister's boyfriend first. You'd know him if I said his name. He wanted me to have the abortion and so I did. I was that kind of a person then, do what the man says. I've felt guilty ever since; it's not exactly a nunny thing to do, have an abortion.

My brother Roy is going to die next, if Albert doesn't beat him to it. They both have cancer. Roy is alone like me, never married. I will take care of Roy; do whatever he needs. It's a deal I made with God: I take care of Roy, God forgives me for the abortion. I can't forgive myself, of course, but that's just part of being a Catholic, dragging all that guilt behind you, right into the grave, I would guess.

But now it's time for my treat for the day, *Wheel of Fortune*. Time to get out the Old English and the dust rag. I can't just sit there and watch the show like a normal person would. I dust and listen to the show, try to solve the puzzles while I work. And wish I looked a little like Vanna. Bet nobody ever called her husky.

[She walks toward living room.]

Curtain

CAROL WOBIG

7 A TWIST IN THE BRAIN

"Guess what?" Kenny jiggled his Christmas gift, his own set of measuring spoons, against his thigh.

"What?" I asked.

"Aliens visited me last night."

"Aliens? Real aliens?"

"Yeah, they were real." He sat down at the table and sprinkled a perfect tablespoon of sugar onto his cereal.

I leaned against the counter, drank my coffee, and tried to think of what a good mother's response to this news would be.

"Were the aliens friendly?" I asked, deciding to enter into his fantasy. I read that in a child-rearing book from the Goodwill store.

"Sort of." He took his first bite of cereal and smiled up at me. "Ah," he said. "I feel better."

I raised my coffee cup to him, our morning routine. His knuckles were a mess of chapped skin and tiny red scabs. The hand washing was back. It started at the beginning of first grade, stopped in the spring, started up again this fall.

Last month, before he started second grade, we took a step up in the world and moved out of the basement at my folks' place and into The Pine Cone Mobile Home Park. Our trailer was the third on the right, the one with Duct Tape holding the screens in place.

After breakfast we waited at the end of the driveway for the bus. "See you tonight," I said.

He climbed up into the bus, found his seat and waved to me. I used to blow him a kiss, but he asked me not to do that anymore.

My job was at the tavern across the road. I know, probably not the best job for an alkie, a former alkie, but bartending was all I knew and Edna needed help. Her husband of fifty-two years had died in his sleep a few months earlier and she was almost as desperate as I was.

She opened the bar at six a.m. to catch the third shift people on their way home from the pizza factory, and I took over after Kenny was on the bus. I just ran across the two-lane and was at work. First I made coffee and then I woke up Terry. He stopped every morning, drank three beers, put his head down on the bar and slept for a couple of hours while Edna watched the *Today Show.*

"So, help me out," I said to Terry when I saw that he was coming to. I was down on my knees loading bottles of beer into the cooler behind the bar. Just holding the neck of the bottle made me long to pop one open.

"What's up?" He held a cup of coffee close to his nose and inhaled the steam.

"Kenny tells me that aliens are visiting in his sleep." He laughed, inhaled more steam.

"Don't laugh. I'm worried sick about him. He's washing his hands again."

"It's just a phase. Kids go through phases. Mickey slept on the floor next to my bed for awhile last year." He blew his nose in napkins from the stack on the edge of the bar.

I stood up and stretched my back. I kept my eyes on the napkins in Terry's hands. "Did Mickey get over it?"

"Sure." He blew again.

"Take those napkins with you."

"I always do, don't I?"

"Yes, but there might be that one time you forget." I searched through the shelves behind the bar for the feather duster.

He put the napkins into his pocket. "Okay?"

"Good job, Terrence." I dusted his place at the bar.

"Time for me to go," he said and slid off the stool

and put on his jacket.

"Did Mickey ever do the hand washing thing?"

"No, I have to drag him into the bathroom to clean up."

"That's what I mean. It isn't normal. And now the aliens."

He walked to the door, held it open, and let in a shaft of light and a blast of cold air.

"Just ignore him. He'll get over it." The door closed behind him.

AT TEN, EDNA came out of her apartment behind the bar. I knew what her mood was by her dress. Today, a good day, she'd combed her hair and wore a sweatshirt and jeans. Bad days, she worked with a scarf tied over the rollers in her hair, wore one of Ed's flannel shirts on top of her bathrobe, and shuffled off to the back room for a nap when it was slow. She hoisted herself up to her place at the end of the bar.

"You can cut those smaller," she said, nodding at the limes I was slicing for the lunch rush.

I cut the ones in front of me in half again. "Have you noticed any change in Kenny?" I asked. After school, he stayed in the back with her until my shift was over.

"His knuckles look chapped, but otherwise he seems to be okay."

"This morning he told me he's seeing aliens in his

sleep." I wanted a beer so bad, but sucked on a lime instead.

She held her cup out to me for a refill. "You should call that stupid husband of yours. That's what you should do. He should be helping you."

"I know," I said.

"Do we need anything?" she asked.

"Miller Lite."

She ran her pink fingernail down the list of phone numbers written on the wall next to her stool and dialed the Miller distributor.

AFTER THE LUNCH RUSH, I called Sam, my soon-to-be ex.

"I need to talk to you."

"I don't have any money," he said.

I took a deep breath, stopped myself from slamming down the phone. "It's not about money, it's about Kenny."

"What's the little brat done now? Robbed a bank?"

"No, he's smarter than you are." The TV in the background got louder. "He's washing his hands again. And yesterday, he told me aliens visited him during the night."

"Look, I'd like to help you, but in case you haven't heard, I've got my own problems."

"Maybe you could spend a little time with him?"

"You want the jerk you're getting rid of to spend more time with him?" The volume on the TV went up higher. "Anyway, I can't leave the house until my trial."

"You're still his father." I twisted my fingers around the phone cord.

"And how would I know that for sure?"

"You ass," I said and hung up. Kenny looked just like him, the sweet shape of his lips, the straight black eyebrows. For a while, I loved them both.

AFTER MY SHIFT, I went back to Edna's apartment. She and Kenny, squeezed into her recliner, were asleep. Cheese-encrusted microwave trays sat on the end table. I pulled Kenny out of his nest without waking Edna, stood him up and wrapped him in his jacket, loaded him and his backpack on my shoulder, and went out the back door. When the cold hit he burrowed his head into my neck.

"You awake, baby?" I stood by the road and waited for two sets of headlights to pass.

"No." He burrowed in deeper.

When I got close to our trailer, I heard the wind slap the drooping roll-up awning on Kenny's window against the metal siding. Maybe that was what he heard in the night. I'd ask Terry to fix it. Inside, I laid him in my bed, the pull-out couch in the living room. His own bed was surrounded with Star Wars posters. Maybe that was what he was seeing in the night.

I decided to ignore the quivering light on the answering machine for a while. I did the dishes, read the paper, worked the crossword.

Kenny moaned. I stretched out on the bed and pulled him close to me. When he was quiet again, I took his left hand out from under the blanket and looked at it in the light from the kitchen. He'd let me cover the scabs with ointment, but then was in the bathroom washing it off when he thought I wasn't looking.

When the hand washing came back, the measuring started, too. I didn't fight that. Maybe he would be a carpenter, make a lot of money. I bought him two measuring tapes and a new notebook for his birthday. By Christmas, he'd measured everything in the house over and over, written it all down in dated columns in the notebook.

Before I fell asleep, I reached over to the end table and played the message.

"Mrs. Weber, I need to talk to you." His teacher. She had noticed his knuckles. Would I come in for a meeting?

She knew me, knew my family. I pulled him closer to me, tucked the blanket up around his neck. If I went to see Mrs. Sandowski, she would tell me I'm a bad mother. If I didn't go, she would call the social services. Oh, for a beer.

THE NEXT NIGHT, when I went to the back to Edna's apartment to pick him up, Kenny was asleep on the couch. I sat next to his feet and tickled him awake. He sat up and nuzzled into my side.

"Sounded like business was good tonight," Edna said. Some nights, she made herself stay awake to root for her favorite on *American Idol.*

"Not bad," I said. "Can Edna hear about the aliens?" I asked Kenny before he nodded off again.

"I think so."

"I used to have aliens visit me," Edna said. She kept her eyes on the TV.

"You did?" Kenny pulled away from me and sat on the edge of the couch. "What did they look like?"

"Well, they were the old-time kind of aliens. They looked like farmers, wore straw hats and overalls. They each carried a hoe."

I buried my face in the collar of my coat, swallowed my laughter.

"What did their faces look like?"

"Um, like pears." Now she had both of us hooked. "Yes, pears." She snuck a glance at us. A young woman was on the stage singing her guts out.

We waited for the commercial.

"Yes, big pears," she said. "Their cheeks bulged out around their mouths. I saw their pointed heads only once. The night they took their hats off."

"Why did they do that?" Kenny asked.

"Let me think." Her second most favorite contestant was singing. We waited.

"Oh, they took their hats off the night they said goodbye. They told me their work was done. That I didn't need them anymore."

"They helped you?" I asked.

"Oh, yes. They helped me a lot. They taught me how to read."

"No way," Kenny said.

"They did. Got all that phonics stuff into my hard head." A commercial came on. "Come over here."

He stood next to the raised footrest of her recliner, lowered his right hand to her lumpy ankle.

"What do your aliens look like?" Edna asked.

I tightened my jacket over my chest.

He moved his fingers back and forth on her ankle. "Their heads are circles. They have eyes and mouths, but no noses."

"Well that's convenient. Never have to blow it. Have they said what they want?" I leaned forward.

"They want me to go with them."

"To their house?"

He nodded.

"I think that would be okay," Edna said.

"You do?" I said.

"Yes, I think it would be fun, to see where they live.

But just for a visit. Right?"

"I think so," Kenny said.

"Sure. I went and visited mine all the time. They lived in the hayloft. That's where I studied. Now get out of here, I have to watch my show."

From the tavern parking lot, we saw that all the letters on the neon sign for the trailer park were lit up, even the pinecone.

"Do you think the aliens have a sign in front of their house?" Kenny asked.

"You'll have to let me know." We ran across the road. The drooping awning had been rolled up and tied with a piece of clothes line. *Thank you, Terry.*

IN THE MORNING, we went through our usual routine, until it was time to leave. Kenny wouldn't get up from the table.

"Are you sick?" I put my hand on his forehead.

"I don't want to go to school anymore."

"Were the aliens back?"

"No."

Now what? I knelt down next to him, rubbed his back, kissed his ear. "You have to go to school. I go to work. You go to school. What's wrong?"

"Mrs. Sandowski won't let me wash my hands when I need to." He pushed his cereal bowl forward and put his head down on the table.

I sat back on my heels. Please, please help me, I prayed. Please. "How about if I get Edna to give me a ride up to the school this afternoon. I'll talk to Mrs. Sandowski."

"Okay." He wiped his nose on his sleeve. The cleanliness thing only applied to his hands.

"Can you make it through today?" I thought I might be acting like the AA counselor I never went to see.

"If you promise to be there after school."

"I promise," I said, and remembered the night he sat at my sister's with his coat on for six hours, waiting for me to show up. "I'll be there."

EDNA DROVE ME up to the school.

"Do you want me to come in with you?" she asked.

"What do you think would be the best thing to do?"

"I'll go to the grocery store. You'll do fine." She turned her head and smiled at me. I teared up, something I don't often do.

"Okay."

She dropped me off behind the line of idling buses in front of the school. Mrs. Sandowski, in a long green coat, gave orders to the kids. Her gray hair flew around her red face. Kenny leaned against the building, kicked at a patch of ice.

"Oh, you came," she said. "Kenny told me you were coming."

"I'm here," I said.

"Mom!" Kenny ran up to me.

I hugged him. Pulled his hat down over his ears.

"You two can wait in my room," Mrs. Sandowski said.

The school smelled the same: floor wax mixed with wet boots and forgotten baloney sandwiches. Kenny showed me around his room. The guinea pig. The books along the shelf under the window. His math paper on the bulletin board.

"Kenny does a fine job in math," Mrs. Sandowski said when she came in. "Have a seat."

I crunched myself into the desk in front of her.

"Kenny, would you take this to the office for me?" She handed him an envelope. "And you can stop and wash your hands on the way back."

He smiled at her like she'd just given him a new tape measure.

"Mrs. Weber," she said, "Kenny is—"

"I'm doing my best to make this work," I said. "I go to work every day. We have a place to live. It's been two years since I've touched any alcohol or drugs."

"I know you've turned your life around." Her clasped hands rested on a book sitting on the desk in front of her.

"You do? How do you know that?"

"I called Edna. We went to school together."

I released my sweaty hands from the edge of the desk.

"What I want to tell you before Kenny gets back is that he has a disease."

"A disease? What kind of a disease?" Besides the hand washing and the measuring he has a disease?

"It's called OCD. I want you to read this book and get some help for him." She slid the book toward the edge of the desk.

"What about the hand washing?" I asked holding the book in my hands.

She smiled. "That is the disease, Mrs. Weber. The hand washing, the measuring. Obsessive Compulsive Disorder. Researchers have found that these kids have a twist in their brain that may cause these behaviors. Kenny's measured every inch of this room. Asks me to stay in at recess every day so he can check his numbers. I have to push him out the door."

"Washing his hands and measuring is a disease? I thought it was because I was a bad mother."

"You probably were a bad mother at one time," she said.

I couldn't argue with her.

"But this isn't your fault."

"Really?"

"Really. I talked to a doctor and she's willing to work with Kenny. There are medications that help. I'm going to give you a number to call."

Kenny came back into the room, stood next to me and leaned into my shoulder.

"Kenny," she said, "give this to your mother." I took the paper from his damp hand.

"Tomorrow, Kenny, I want you to bring me in a list of when you think you'll want to wash your hands. I'll check off the times when it's okay. Do you think that would work?"

He grinned and nodded. I thought of all the times I'd called her Mrs. Sandowski the cowski, and regretted my smart-ass ways.

"So, you put in a good word for me," I said to Edna on the ride home.

"I did. How did it go?"

I turned the title of the book toward her, pretending to wash my hands low in my lap so Kenny didn't see it. "It's a disease," I mouthed to her. She didn't understand me.

I held the book up and ran my finger under the word disease, hoping we didn't end up in the ditch. "Really?" She glanced at me for a second.

"She gave me a number to call."

"How about that." Edna said, "I was worried."

"Me, too," I said and looked back at Kenny. He was writing something in his notebook.

THE NEXT MORNING, he ate his Cheerios and finished his hand-washing list. From across the table, I could see that he was up to ten trips to the rest room, was adding an eleventh.

"Did the aliens visit last night?" I had stayed up all night and read the book. Maybe he did have a disease. Maybe I did, too.

He nodded and added twelve and thirteen to his list.

"I went to their house."

"No way," I said, and took a deep breath. "And what was the house like?"

"It was a double-wide." The fourteenth hand washing went on the list.

"A double-wide? They must be rich."

He looked up at me. "They let me measure the whole thing. They had an extra long tape measure. It glowed in the dark. Do you think I could have one like that?"

"Don't see why not. The bills are paid." He added one more hand washing to the list. Fifteen.

"Time to go," he said, and folded up his list and put it into his pocket. I put the phone number Mrs. Sandowski had given me into mine and we headed down the driveway to wait for the bus.

CAROL WOBIG

8 Poached Is Not an Option

Bobby Jr. and I stood on the sidewalk, arms crossed over our chests, and looked at his van. Rust crawled over the black vehicle like a fungus. Jack's Plumbing and Heating was painted over, almost hidden by a stenciled "Jesus Saves." Drips of paint ran down from the J and S.

"Have you been saved?" I asked. He'd just driven up from Florida to surprise me. That had worked.

"Sort of," he said. "What about you?"

"Me saved? No, I just prayed that my hair would grow back."

We laughed.

"Where should I park?" he asked.

"In the garage. I'll park on the street."

"I don't want to put you out," he said. He had to take off his cowboy hat to fit into the van. "I'll park next to the driveway."

Please put me out, I thought, lit up and checked to see if my neighbor Thelma was peering out of her window. "Where's Jenny?" I asked before he drove onto my lawn.

"Don't ask," he said.

No wife, a junker van, and a cowboy outfit? Not only was he wearing a black cowboy hat on his shaved head, his newly acquired belly hung over tight jeans that led down to pencil-toed boots. He had always dressed up as a cowboy for Halloween.

"So, what's the plan?" I asked when he came into the kitchen.

"Shelly's," he said

"Shelly's?"

"I've wanted one of her pizzas for days."

"We'll walk," I said. "You need the exercise."

"And you need to quit smoking."

"It's like pizza for me," I said and took a long drag from the cigarette in my hand.

"You're sick," he said, "funny, but sick."

Shelly's Shalet smelled the same. Beer, smoke—pain. She stood at the register, her back to the door. Our eyes met in the mirror. She raised her eyebrows and I headed off to the table in the farthest corner, next to the fake fireplace that glowed in the July humidity.

Bobby ordered an extra large pepperoni and sausage pizza, a beer for him and white wine for me. "Shelly's looking old," I said.

"She looks the same to me."

"She can't. She's close to my age."

"Guess I didn't notice," he said and kept eating, ate the whole pizza.

My phone rang. Mackenzie.

"Your sister." I handed him the phone.

"Up here on vacation," he said.

Vacation? For how long?

He closed the phone and handed it back to me. "She'll be up in the morning."

"She didn't get my permission," I said and felt my pocket to make sure I had my smokes.

"She has to ask permission?"

"Sort of," I said. He didn't ask why. The three of us weren't good at getting to the bottom of things.

He got up and fed a handful of coins into the juke box.

"Play some Everly Brothers, would you? If it's still on there?" I teared up when "All I Have To Do Is Dream" came over the speakers, but before I completely fell apart, Shelly was standing in front of me, her bleached hair spread out in crispy waves beneath a green fedora. Cute, too cute. Her hips had spread out, too.

"Eunice, nice to see you."

I'll bet. I moved my wine glass round and round on its soggy napkin.

"Can I get you a refill? On the house?"

I nodded. The pizza had put me way over my calorie count for the day, might as well go for it.

She returned with a wine for me, a beer for Bobby and a cup of coffee for herself. "So, it's been a long time."

"Thirty-two years."

"Bobby sure looks like his dad." She poured three creamers into her coffee.

He was plugging more coins into the juke box.

"Not too much, I hope. Big Bobby died last year."

"Heart attack?" she asked and turned and waved to a couple coming in the door.

"Cancer," I said.

"Me, too," she said and squeezed her left breast. "This is as fake as the fireplace."

I had to laugh, and pushed my left arm against my own breast, made sure it was still there.

A baseball team, loud and dirty, still in uniform and cleats, walked in the door.

"Gotta go," she said.

When the team's celebration of their win drowned out the music, we left.

"So what was the story with Shelly?" Bobby asked when we crossed Center Street. "Dad would never tell me."

"I guess you're old enough for the truth," I said. "They had an affair."

"Dad?"

"Yeah. We used to put you in the stroller, walk up there, have a few beers, walk home. But when Mackenzie came along I stayed home."

"And?"

We were home now, standing next to his van. I moved over to the "Jesus Saves" sign and picked at a dribble of paint that hung from the S.

"Your dad still went and soon I was hearing rumors about him and Shelly. One night I got a baby sitter and investigated for myself."

"And?"

"And I looked in the front window of the bar and saw them dancing. Tight. Like lovers. I marched right in. I was like that in those days." I kept picking at the paint.

"And?" He started to pick at a drip from the J.

"When they saw me, they jumped away from each other like kids caught with their pants down. I blew. At one point I called him Big Bobby with the little—well, I won't repeat what I said—but that was the end as far as I was concerned. I thought they'd get married, my next humiliation, but they didn't. Both moved on to other lucky people."

"Well," he said and unlocked his van, "how about a cup of tea? We'll finish picking in the morning." We laughed.

The van was neat as a pin. That, he got from me.

"Sit here," he said and gestured toward a bunk.

He knelt on the floor in front of his kitchen area and turned on a battery operated teapot. A wooden box that held a crucifix and a votive candle hung from the back of the driver's seat. What looked like a Bible lay open beneath the shrine.

"So," I said and dipped the tea bag up and down, up and down, "what happened with you and Jenny?"

"Same thing as you and Dad," he said, after a few dips of his tea bag. "Only it was a woman."

"Ouch," I said. "Pain's the same, I imagine."

"Oh, yeah. I've got a belly's worth of it here," he said and patted his stomach.

We laughed.

"You know, you can sleep in the house," I said.

"This is fine. I'm used to it."

AT THREE A.M., I was up wandering the house. Bobby was up, too. A light flickered through the madras spread he used to cover the windows. I pictured him kneeling in front of his shrine, candle burning, praying. For himself? For me? I hoped he was praying for a plan to come to him, one other than living in the driveway. I loved my kids, but didn't want them living with me again.

And Mackenzie was coming up in the morning. Poor Mackenzie. My twit child. Nothing suited her from day one. I had to drag her to first grade one day even though her socks didn't feel right to her. And the food problem. Corn flakes and donuts. You wouldn't think a child could survive on that, but she did.

Now it was men. She wanted to be married but couldn't find the right guy. The last time she was up here, I lost my temper and made it her fault.

"There is no guy out there good enough for you," I yelled at her and told her she was selfish and needed to grow up and shouldn't come back until I said it was okay.

It was 3:18 and I lit up. Just one. I charged it to Saturday's quota, and went back to bed.

IN THE MORNING, I was in the basement doing Bobby's laundry, hoping that the phone would ring and it would be Mackenzie canceling her visit, when I heard footsteps on the floor above me.

"Where are you?"

"Down here, I'll be right up." I started to transfer Bobby's clothes to the dryer when I saw her boots on the stairs, then her ironed jeans, her skinny body. We were clones except for my sags and bags, though her jeans did look a little snug. After dusting off the middle step, she sat down.

"So you're doing his laundry."

"Guilty as charged," I said. Her brother was my favorite as far as she was concerned. Usually as far as I was concerned, too.

"And that monstrosity parked in the yard?" She handed me a folded piece of notebook paper. "This was in the door."

"His new home," I said and turned over a bucket, sat down next to the dryer, and read the note.

I hope that thing will be moved sooner rather than later.

Thelma

Mackenzie didn't ask what the note said or who it was from, or anything about her brother, or me.

"Jake told me last week that he wants to move out," she said and lowered her head onto her knees.

Here we go. The long ringlets of her hair trembled as she wept. Bobby's jeans thumped and clicked in the dryer. The day loomed ahead of me, a twelve-hour counseling session and there would be a fight. There was always a fight when she and Bobby were both home.

"What about the deal we made?" I said and shooed her up the stairs.

"The deal?" She dug a box of chocolate-covered donuts out of her purse.

She was eating donuts? She was usually more obsessive about calories than I was. "You don't visit unless I say I'm up for it?"

"Oh, sorry," she said. "I forgot. You're going to let

Bobby stay here, aren't you, for as long as he likes?"

"That's different." I poured us a cup of coffee.

He came into the kitchen from the shower, reeking of Aqua Velva, his dad's favorite.

"Mackenzie." He gave her a one-armed hug that she pulled away from.

"What a nice surprise," she said and ate a donut.

"So what's your current crisis?" He helped himself to two donuts.

"Probably the same as yours," Mackenzie said, "except I didn't turn myself into a side show."

"Now, now," I said. Spits of hot grease from the bacon I was frying jumped up and burned the back of my hand.

"Mom, why don't you at least broil that?" Mackenzie said. "Aren't you trying to eat better?"

"It's my only sin," I said. She'd freak if she knew I was still smoking.

"So, back to me," Bobby said. "You don't like my new duds?"

"You're too old and fat to be a cowboy," she said and bit into a second donut.

Two donuts? I was shocked.

"Women like it," he said.

"I find that hard to believe," Mackenzie said.

"So, do we want our eggs fried or scrambled?" I asked.

"Whatever my sister wants is fine with me," Bobby said and finished off his second donut.

"Poached," Mackenzie said.

"Poached is not an option," I said. I did have my limits.

"Scrambled," Bobby said.

"And as always you're the one that matters around here," Mackenzie said.

"Let's just have a nice breakfast," I said and cracked eight eggs into a bowl and felt my back tighten up.

One of my mistakes with my daughter, and there were many, was the name I'd chosen for her. Mackenzie was too much for her to live up to. I should have given her my name. What a clunker. I never did understand how my mother could have named a sweet little baby—I was a sweet little baby—Eunice.

"So why didn't your wonderful wife come along with you?" Mackenzie asked and poured us all another cup of coffee.

Bobby looked at me.

"She didn't want to ride in that van for two days," I said and set the food on the table.

"No, no," he said. "We split up."

"Oh, sorry," Mackenzie said.

Bobby told her the story.

"And that turned you into a cowboy?" she asked.

I had to laugh.

"Yup," he said and squirted ketchup onto his eggs.

"And when were you saved?" I asked.

"After."

"And are you planning to save us?" Mackenzie asked.

"Not this time around," he said. "I'm not too sure about it all myself. I'm just giving it a try."

"Well, that's a relief," I said.

"You need to be saved, Mom," Mackenzie said, "still smoking after cancer."

"I'm not."

"You are. I can smell it."

"Okay. I am."

"You have to quit."

"Let's just eat," I said.

When we were finished, I picked up the plates, loaded them into the dishwasher.

"You do have to quit smoking," Mackenzie said, "or I won't be able to come and visit."

Not exactly an unhappy ultimatum in my book. "And why would that be?"

"You can't smoke around my baby," she said.

"Your baby? You're pregnant?" My twit child, pregnant?

"Sort of."

"You can't be sort of pregnant," I said, not knowing whether I wanted it to be true or not.

"You're kidding," Bobby said and checked to make

sure that the donut box was empty.

"No, it's true." She reached into the satchel she called a purse and pulled out more donuts and an ultrasound photograph. She set it on the table and we all leaned in for a look. "Mackenzie Richards" was typed on the bottom edge.

"Is it a boy or a girl?" I asked.

"She's a girl, not an it."

"And Jake?"

"He says he's not ready to be a father." So, she would be on her own.

There was a knock at the door. Thelma. "Could somebody open this for me?" She pressed a bottle of fiery red nail polish into the screen.

"Come on in," Bobby said. "We're celebrating."

"Oh yeah?" She sat down at the table. "What's the occasion?"

Mackenzie cracked open her second box of donuts. Powdered sugar this time. I started wiping the bacon grease off the top of the stove.

"Mom's going to be a grandma."

"That's great," Thelma said. "Grandchildren are the best. When they're making you crazy, you just send them home."

"My child will be just like me, perfect," Mackenzie said.

"Right," Bobby said. "Let me open that for you, Thelma."

"Great color," Mackenzie said. "Slide your hand over here."

I turned around. Mackenzie was painting Thelma's nails. Bobby was studying the ultrasound photograph, holding a half-eaten donut off to the side.

"Have you picked a name?" I asked.

"Eunice," she said and drew a swath of red on Thelma's pinky finger.

"Are you nuts?" I said. "You will not name your baby Eunice."

"I will if I want to," she said. "She's my baby."

"No, you will not," I said and took out my cigarettes and knocked one into my hand.

Thelma held her finished nails up in front of her and smiled at them. "Those notes," she said to me, "forget about them. I was having a bad day."

"Okay," I said.

"You're next," Mackenzie said to me.

I sat down and spread my left hand out on a napkin, still held the cigarette in my right.

"Tell her that naming her baby Eunice will be a sin," I said to Bobby.

"Thou shalt not name thy baby Eunice."

"Middle-aged fat guys shalt not dress like cowboys."

I laughed, and liked both of them, for the moment. Thelma sat and smiled at her fingernails. Bobby dusted powdered sugar off his t-shirt.

"Get your right hand up here," Mackenzie said.

"Just a minute," I said, "I need a break."

I went out on the porch and lit up, lifted the cigarette to my lips, inhaled once, dropped it to the cement and crushed it out. My last, I knew it was my last.

"So, about that little girl's name," I said when I was inside again. "It will not be Eunice."

"It will," Mackenzie said. Here we go.

9 LEARNING TO DRIVE

"Ruby," Agnes yelled from her bedroom, "get in here."

"In a minute," I said. It was early June. I was finishing up the supper dishes and wanted to get them done so I could sit out in the back yard and watch the fireflies before the mosquitoes arrived.

"Ruby!" she yelled louder this time. "Get in here."

I hurried into the bedroom. She sat at her dressing table, naked from the waist up.

"Feel this," she said.

We were twins, had lived together all our lives in our folks' four unit, but I'd never seen her breasts before. To my surprise, when not held in place by her frilly bra, they looked just like mine: a fold of empty skin with a nipple that pointed to the floor. Our eyes met in the mirror.

"Oh, don't be silly," Agnes said and took my hand in hers and guided it to a hard lump beneath her skin.

"Must be a cyst," I said. "We'll call Aunt Millie." Millie was the female problems expert in the family, had cysts all the time.

"But it's hard," Agnes said.

"Cysts can be hard," I said, though I had no idea if that was true. I called Millie. "Go to the doctor," she said.

So Agnes took the next Friday off from Webb's, though she hated to since it was the best day for tips. We went to see Doctor Jeff, the son of our folks' doctor. We used to babysit for him.

"I suppose he'll have to examine me," she said and tied the strings of the hospital gown into tight bows.

"Just close your eyes," I said. "Pretend you don't know him." It was easy for me to tell her what to do. I wasn't the one going through this, though just being in the waiting room was a trial: lots of women, some kind of green underneath their skin, wearing scarves over their heads, or shiny wigs.

"Agnes," Doctor Jeff said, when he walked into the exam room. "And Ruby."

We chit-chatted for a bit about the old days and then he asked Agnes to get up on the table. I sat in the chair by the desk and focused on his shoes. They were

soft brown leather, cracked near the ball of his foot
and in need of new heels. The frayed cuffs of his pants
dragged on the floor.

"Is it cancer?" Agnes asked after he examined her.

"It could be," he said and took her hand and helped
her sit up. "But try not to worry too much. Let's
see what the tests say. And if it is, there are lots of
treatments that work these days."

Try not to worry too much. That was a joke.

THE MANAGER AT WEBB'S said Agnes could come back
when she got better. At first we stopped for a BLT after
her chemo, but when her hair fell out she wouldn't go
there anymore. Instead, we went to the Greek place by
the hospital where she didn't know anybody. We'd have
a hamburger and a piece of pie, until eating got to be a
trial for her. Driving became a trial, too.

She'd always been the driver. My dad taught her,
and tried to teach me, but I couldn't get the feel for
the clutch. I could see that it was breaking his heart
to have me lurching up and down the driveway in his
new Buick, so I gave it up. Agnes drove. I rode along
or took the bus.

One night, after a day of chemo, as we watched *CSI:
NY*—not as good as *CSI: MIAMI*, but a distraction
nonetheless—Agnes handed me a piece of paper. It was
a list, a To Do list for me: learn how to drive, how to

balance the checkbook, and rent the apartments.

"You can still drive," I said.

"I'm dying," she said. She said this all the time.

"You're not dying," I said to the TV, though the thought had crossed my mind. For sure she was disappearing.

"Now, I can drive, but when I'm gone, you need to be able to take care of yourself."

"You're not going anywhere," I said, "and I can still walk." I set the list on the end table. I would have gone to bed, but had to see how the program ended.

"And why do we need to rent the apartments?" I asked at the next commercial break. They'd been empty for a year. We didn't like the noise of other people in the building.

She muted the TV. "You'll need the money. To take care of yourself. You're not going to live forever either."

"Turn up the sound," I said. The show was back on.

I STEWED OVER THE LIST for a day or two, and finally walked down the street to the driving school. It was on 74th in what used to be Joe's Barber Shop.

"Can you teach an old lady how to drive?" I asked the young man behind the counter.

He looked me over. "How are your eyes?"

"Still work," I said and read the fine print for him on the application sitting on the counter.

"We'll give it a try then," he said.

So there I was the next day in the back seat of a little car with a sign on the back that said Student Driver. A teen-age boy sat next to me — so far we hadn't talked to each other — and a teen-age girl drove. The instructor sat in front of me. I was scared to death.

"Rule One," the instructor said, "seat belts."

"I never wear 'em," the boy said.

"You can wear it, Jason, or get out," the instructor said.

The boy clicked his belt into place. I wanted to tell him how my folks had died, but refrained.

"Thank you," the instructor said into the rearview mirror. "Turn the key, Tiffany."

Tiffany, what a pretty name, so much softer than Ruby and Agnes. She did okay, but I couldn't relax. Once when she hit the brakes at a corner, I grabbed Jason's arm.

"Sorry," I said.

He moved closer to the door.

I thought he'd be next to drive, but the instructor had Tiffany pull over on a side street and told me it was my turn. I almost backed out, but then I thought if someone named Tiffany could learn to drive, I guess I could at least give it a try. The automatic transmission made all the difference. I only scared the instructor once. "Slow down," he kind of yelled. Tiffany and Jason laughed.

On the walk home, I thought about all the times I hadn't done things I'd wanted to do because I couldn't drive or couldn't get there on the bus. Sometimes Agnes wouldn't be in the mood for a movie I wanted to see, or didn't want to go to the cemetery and put flowers on the folks' grave. In the end, I let her run the show. I could have moved out, made my own life, but I was afraid, always afraid. What would happen now, I wondered, if she really did die?

When I got home from the driving school, the door to the folks' apartment was open—we hadn't rented it out after they died—and Agnes was up on a chair taking down the drapes.

"What are you doing?"

"These have to go," she said and dropped another panel to the floor. Dust rose up into the afternoon sunshine.

"They're perfectly good," I said.

"Look at this," she said and pushed a painted nail right through a pleat. "And the carpet. That has to go, too." She'd moved the throw rugs. The carpet was worn right down to the bare floor.

"Do we have the money for this?" I asked over and over again in the next days when I heard her on the phone to Sears ordering more work done.

"That's why you need to do the bills," she said.

I really could have done that all those years, but she brought home the money so I figured she'd like to know where it went. She gave me an allowance, with a raise now and then. It worked.

So the folks' apartment that had been empty for years was remodeled, the upstairs units that had been empty for months were cleaned one more time. I drove—yes I did get my license—up to the Home Depot and bought a For Rent sign.

I interviewed applicants and rented the upstairs units right away, but couldn't seem to find the right person for the folks' place.

"What is the problem?" Agnes asked me one night. She was lying on the couch, barely visible under the down comforter she wanted wrapped around her day and night. I slept in the recliner, right next to her, to keep her covered. The TV, on all the time, flashed in the darkness. I pushed the mute button.

"I'm not sure," I said to her, though earlier in the day when I took an applicant on a tour, the answer came to me. I wanted to move over there, but I didn't want to tell her. It just seemed too sad, that after she was gone, I could be living in that beautiful new apartment.

"Well," she said, and burrowed deeper into her

cocoon, "you can drive, the upstairs is rented, when you quit being so picky the downstairs will be rented. I guess I can die now."

In the past, I'd always joked with her. You don't have to die, I would say. We would laugh. But that night I couldn't get the words out.

She lasted three more months.

Afterwards, the emptiness was overwhelming. A hundred times a day I'd think of things I wanted to tell her when she got home from work. Her quilt was still on the couch. I still slept in the recliner, and I kept showing the empty apartment to people and turning them down. In between, I sat in my chair and watched TV, until the day I drove over to the cemetery and our marker was finally in place. We'd picked it out together and had it engraved with a bouquet of flowers and our names:

Agnes Muenster, Sept. 1942-2008
Ruby Muenster, Sept. 1942- _____

I laid the flowers I'd bought at Pick 'n Save on the stone. It was cold, light snow fell, the flowers would be frozen in an hour or two, but she loved flowers.

On the drive home, I couldn't get the sight of my name on the marker out of my head. When I got home, before I even took off my coat, I called Sears and ordered a leather recliner for myself, one I'd been looking at every week in the Sunday paper. And then I called Two Men and a Truck.

"It'll be an easy move," I said, "just across the hall."

CAROL WOBIG

10 Happy Thanksgiving

Gwen joined her son and his boyfriend at Benny's Hideaway on Wednesday for a night out of the house. A banner taped to the mirror behind the bar invited everyone to a Thanksgiving Buffet the next day at 6:30 p.m. It rose and fell each time someone walked in. She sat on the bar stool closest to the door, her fat body drenched from a hot flash. Such a curse. Her son Evan, 6'2" now, stood next to her, stooping a bit, so she could braid his long red hair, the same color as hers, into a ponytail. "Sure you don't want to come here tomorrow?" she asked.

"I thought you wanted to go to the farm," he said.

"I do," she said, though she didn't.

"And Richie's never been on a farm. He wants to see it."

She wrapped the end of her son's braid in a gold

tie and gave it a tug. "Okay, that's what we'll do then."

As the band started playing, Richie, the current boyfriend, a sliver of a young man dressed in black, came out of the rest room and danced toward them in the mirror. Evan raised up his long torso and pushed his silky green shirt into his tight pants and laughed. "He's a wild man."

The boys, they were all boys to her, danced in the mirror behind the liquor bottles lined up in front of her. She picked at the damp label of her bottle of Miller Lite, stopping every so often to inspect the tips of her manicured nails, a luxury she could afford since Evan was out on his own. She did not want to go up to the farm.

IN THE MORNING, Evan drove, Richie slept in the passenger seat snoring softly, and Gwen rode in the back, snacking. When they turned onto Hwy. 28, she leaned forward, her mouth close to Evan's ear, "Have you told Richie what kind of man your grandfather is?"

"More or less," Evan said. He reached up and squeezed her fingers gripping the headrest of his seat. "Everything will be okay."

Gwen sat back and fluffed her skirt, sending crumbs from the chips and muffin she'd eaten to the floor. The elastic of her knee-hi hose (why hadn't she worn pants) dug into the soft flesh behind her knees. She cracked the window for a little air, took deep breaths, closed her eyes until she felt the car slow down, turn. A sign advertising wood for sale was nailed to the tree closest to the end of the driveway. Her dad had sold the herd in the spring. Now he was selling the barn, piece by piece, as were so many Wisconsin farmers.

Evan parked the car. He and Richie got out, stretched, and admired her brother Bill's Harley, while Gwen sat in the back seat with the door open, catching her breath, again. She had to do this. Everything would be okay. Down the hill to the right, the foundation of the barn stood open to the sky, its paned windows and silo still intact. The wood that used to be the hayloft, sorted into lengths, lay in two long rows in the front yard. A huge roll of twine, scissors protruding from its center, sat on the stump near the front porch. She and her sister Julie had loved that stump, the center of all their playing-house fantasies. Julie's daughters came running out the back door in pink puffy jackets, followed by her sister. Gwen forced herself out of the car. She hugged Julie, a long one. They were the only members in their family who dared to hug one another. "Should we turn around and go home?"

"No, no," Julie said. "Stay. He's watching football. We'll just ignore him."

She and Julie walked back to the house. Evan and Richie pushed the girls high into the air on the swings that still hung from the branches of twin oaks she and Julie had named Betty and Veronica, after characters they'd discovered in a stash of comic books in the attic.

"You're looking good," Julie said.

"I'm trying," Gwen said. Sort of. But it was Thanksgiving.

IN THE KITCHEN, dinner was almost ready. Her mother stood at the stove stirring the gravy. Brother Bill carved the turkey, his manly duty. Gwen mashed the potatoes with a mixer, as perspiration traced a path from her armpits to her bra. She raised the inside window and lifted the slat of wood covering the air holes in the storm, leaned into the cold air, let it seep through her clothes and find her chest, her neck, her face. The football crowd's shouts drifted in from the living room.

Her mother set the roasting pan in the sink and squeezed a blob of Dawn into the water, leaned over Gwen, and closed the window. "You know how Dad is about the heating bill."

"Oh, I forgot," Gwen said. She'd forgotten nothing.

"Who is that young man with Evan?" her mother asked. "I think they're swinging the girls too high."

"They're just having fun," Gwen said. "You worry too much."

"I know. I know. You loved to swing. I always knew where to find you when things calmed down."

Gwen cleaned off the beaters, worked a spoon through the still lumpy potatoes. "I guess we all survived," she said.

"And none the worse for wear," her mother said as she sloshed the soapy water around the edges of the pan.

None the worse for wear? She had to be kidding. None the worse for wear?

"Who is that young man with Evan?" her mother asked again.

"A friend," Gwen said, and turned on the mixer again. "Just a friend." Gwen's stomach growled. If no one would have noticed, she would have eaten the whole pile of potatoes she was spooning into a bowl, all by herself. With lots of butter.

For a moment the roaring football crowd fell silent, replaced with the squeaking wheels of the TV stand being pushed down the hallway from the living room to the dining room.

"Hi, Dad," Gwen said as she set the potatoes in the center of the table.

"Are we ever going to eat?" he asked. He plugged in the TV, sat at the head of the table, adjusted the antenna, turned up the volume, leaned back and rested his folded arms on his ample belly.

"Any minute now," Gwen said. Take off your stupid

Packer hat she wanted to say, but didn't.

They all sat down, bowed their heads, said grace at their mother's insistence, passed the food. The football crowd cheered on.

"How's your new job going, Dad?" Julie asked.

Gwen slid her eyes over her dad's hands, saw that his cuticles and nails were black with factory grease.

"I hate it," he said, his eyes on the TV. "And these assholes are gonna lose this game. All the money they make and they can't catch the damn ball."

"Dad, the girls," Julie said. "Watch your language."

Gwen tried to relax her shoulders. Evan and Richie and Bill sat across from her, devouring their food.

Her brother sat back and swirled the ice cubes in his Rum and Coke. "Is the wood selling?"

Her dad glanced away from the TV long enough to glare at his son. "It's none of your damn business if the wood is selling. You don't need a loan again, do you?"

"No, just trying to be sociable," Bill said, downing the rest of his drink. "Guess I need another one of these." He went to the kitchen.

"Please, everybody," her mother said from the far end of the table. "It's Thanksgiving. Be nice to one another."

"Great dinner, Ma," Gwen said.

"Looks like you've had one too many great dinners," her father said, not taking his eyes away from the game.

"She's been dieting," Evan said, raising his head up from his plate.

Gwen caught her son's eyes across the table, moved her head from left to right, as in keep your mouth shut, and took another helping of potatoes.

Her dad looked from the TV to Evan. "And what's with that hair hanging off the back of your head?"

"Just a style, Grandpa. I am an artiste, you know." Evan reached for the turkey and loaded up his plate again.

"An artiste?" Her father leaned over his plate. "What does that mean?" He looked from Evan to Richie. "You boys ain't queers are ya? Cause I don't want to be breaking my back in a factory to feed Thanksgiving Dinner to a couple of queers."

"Queers? We're not queers," Evan said. "Just friends. Right Richie?"

"Yes, sir," he said, and bumped Evan's shoulder. "We don't even know what queer means. And thank you for letting us eat your food. Your farm is a beautiful place."

"Used to be," her dad said and turned up the TV. "If it won't dirty your hands too much, I want you and your skinny little buddy to help me stack wood after the game."

"Sure, Grandpa," Evan said.

If she got out of here alive it would be a miracle.

Richie raised his arms and flexed his muscles. "These

arms are scrawny, but you'll be surprised at how much work they can do."

The family laughed; Dad seemed not to notice.

A disaster averted.

The football crowd cheered on.

AFTER DINNER, Gwen stood at the sink, her hands in the dishwater, and watched the boys carry armfuls of wood from the barn to the yard. Her dad supervised. The girls played on the swings, leaned back so that their long hair almost touched the patch of soft dirt below their feet.

"Well, we made it through another one," Julie said, lifting a stack of plates up into the cupboard.

"Why did you bring up his job?" Gwen asked.

"You know me, can't keep my mouth shut. I don't know how you do it."

"What?" Gwen watched her dad walk toward the stump that held the twine and scissors.

"Keep your mouth shut."

He leaned over, took the scissors and slid them in his back pocket.

Gwen turned to look at Julie. "What did you ask me—oh, how do I keep my mouth shut. I keep it shut to him, but open to the food." She took her hands out of the dishwater and grabbed the roll of fat above her waist with both hands. "The words are here."

Julie laughed. She stood next to Gwen. They looked out the window again. "Evan's such a nice kid," she said. "They're good to help Dad after what he said."

"He's such a—my God, what is he doing?" Gwen dropped the silverware she held into the water and ran out of the kitchen, down the porch steps. She lost a clog on the last step and fell onto her right knee, got up and hobbled toward her dad. "Stop," she yelled. "Stop!"

He was dragging Evan backward across the yard by his ponytail, trying to cut it off. Evan held his hair with both hands, jerking his head from side to side. Richie got to them at the same time as Gwen and threw his body, armful of wood and all, against her dad's shoulder. In a clatter of two-by-fours, the three men were on the ground. Evan lay on his back, gasping for breath. Her dad was on his butt, feeling for his hat that had been knocked off and blown away. Richie was on his knees, rubbing his shoulder. Gwen picked up the scissors.

"For God's sake, Dad, what were you doing?"

"No grandson of mine is going to have a goddam ponytail. I can hardly hold my head up in the tavern the way it is. Where's my hat?" He got on his knees, brushed off the seat of his pants, stood up.

Gwen's mother and Bill had come running out of the house.

"Get grandpa's hat," Julie said to one of her girls, cowering behind her.

He grabbed it from his granddaughter, pulled his keys out of his pocket, and walked toward his truck.

"Where are you going?" her mother shouted.

"I'm going to the tavern. While I still can. Before the guys who already think I'm a loser find out that I have a fag grandson." He pulled the brim of his hat closer to his eyes and walked away.

"He's such a stupid son-of-a-bitch." Gwen had heard the tremor in his voice, like the one in her own.

"Don't talk about your father that way," her mother said, looking at her husband driving off in his truck.

"He's not my father." Gwen said. "I'm done with him."

"Wow," Julie said. "It's about time."

Bill started up his Harley, drove slowly down the driveway and waved to all of them. "Happy Thanksgiving," he said.

Gwen gave him the finger.

"You children..." said her mother and went back into the house.

"Are you okay?" Gwen asked Evan.

He sat on the ground, picking hairs from his fingers. "I think so," he said with a wobble in his voice. "He sure took me by surprise. But he didn't get my hair."

Julie handed Gwen her lost clog.

"I couldn't believe what I saw," Richie said, picking

bits of leaves from his black pants. "I thought my family was nuts."

Gwen slipped her foot into her cold shoe. "You looked like a ballet dancer, flying through the air at him with your arms full of wood."

"We fags are good dancers," Richie said, and gave Evan a hand up.

Julie laughed. The girls ran back to the swings.

"Next year, Thanksgiving is at Benny's," Gwen said. "No more of this."

ON THE WAY HOME, after they'd stopped at the custard stand for a hot fudge sundae and were on the road again, Gwen stripped off her hose, wadded them up in a ball and threw them out the window. Evan's eyes met hers in the rearview mirror. He smiled. "Happy Thanksgiving," he said.

She took his ponytail that hung over the seat and gave it a gentle tug. "Happy Thanksgiving."

CAROL WOBIG

11 JUST ONE MORE

It was a Friday afternoon in March, the end of the school day. Roberta's friend Shirley stood in the doorway. "I think we should leave early tomorrow," she said.

"That's fine," Roberta said. "We'll stop for breakfast in Nashotah."

"You still use that pen?" Shirley asked, nodding toward Roberta's hand.

The pen had been a gift from her first class forty years ago. The gold inlay had flaked away, but her professed name remained. She rubbed the pad of her thumb back and forth over the sharp edges of the letters, SR. M. Michaela, O.S.J. "I had to buy a whole case of ink on the internet. One of the kids ordered it for me. It'll last me the rest of my life."

"You are a relic," Shirley said, pulling her sweater

closer to her body and folding her arms across her chest. She leaned into the door jamb.

"I am," Roberta said, "just like this school." It broke her heart that St. Joe's was closing. In the fall, she would be teaching at the new public school, a steel monstrosity taking shape in a cleared cornfield on the East side of town. Probably teaching without Shirley. The blush on her friend's cheekbones matched the pink scarf covering her bald head. Roberta gestured toward the rows of empty desks in front of her. "Why don't you sit down?"

"No, better not," Shirley said. "I'll see you at home." Roberta sat and listened to the click of her friend's heels diminish in the long hallway.

Home for most of their adult lives had been Apartment Three and Four in the Wagner Building. It was two blocks from the school. They left the convent when being a Bride of Christ had lost its luster. They didn't have a car, furniture, or money, but they did have their freedom and a chance at a new life, one that included men, sex, and the big one, love.

Shirley succeeded. She dated men — real men, not only sad former priests, fell in love again and again, almost married.

Roberta failed. She found sex to be a trauma and men irritating. She thought for a while that she might be a lesbian, a word she could only think, not say out loud. But the prospect of crawling into bed with

Shirley, or any woman, didn't feel right either. In the end, she decided she belonged to a third category that didn't have a name, the one that liked to be alone, and she left it at that.

She ran her fingers over the stack of essays in front of her, stood and walked up and down the aisles. She pushed the desks into neat rows, maneuvered the window pole into the hole of the battered frames of the tall windows and closed them, searched the tips of the branches of the maple trees in the side yard for any sign of green.

Back at her desk, still not ready to get down to work, she counted the business cards propped up on a small plastic tray. She had bought them in self-defense, to be able to respond in kind to those thrust at her by angry parents. If she ordered a new batch, she would have to change not only the address but delete the symbol of the Holy Spirit flying about in the left-hand corner. Good riddance to it all. The whole god-thing had deserted her in the last years, just when she could have used it the most. She tossed the remaining cards into the waste basket, and conjured up the refreshing bite of the gin and tonic waiting for her at home. Just one tonight, she told herself and unscrewed the cap of the pen. Just one. She slid the rubber band off of the seniors' essays. Got to work.

IN THE MORNING, Roberta drove. Shirley stretched out in the back seat under a yellow quilt Roberta kept in her car now. They were on their way to visit Mother Theresa. On the seat next to Roberta was a bag with the old woman's favorite foods: Hershey bars, Cheetos, and in a thermos, gin.

"When did we start calling her Tessie?" Shirley asked, adjusting a pillow behind her head.

"Probably when she started treating us like human beings," Roberta said, her eyes in the side view mirror. "But she'll always be Mother Theresa to me." She sped up and merged into the traffic on the highway.

"You're so hard on her," Shirley said. "Being a Mother Superior in the old days was difficult."

"I suppose, but I think she enjoyed being a dictator." Silence. In the rearview mirror she saw that Shirley had closed her eyes.

Roberta reached over and turned on the radio, held the steering wheel with both hands as a semi passed them. Maybe that was what she would do after Shirley died. Be a truck driver. Live on the road. Get a dog to ride along next to her in the cab.

Exit 179. Nashota. At the restaurant in the corner of the Citgo station, she ate breakfast, Shirley nibbled. They bought a bottle of tonic water, a small bag of ice. The nursing home for the old nuns was just up the road.

They found Mother Theresa on the second floor among the wheelchairs surrounding the nurses' station. White-haired heads hung at odd angles, lower lips drooped, glasses were askew.

"Tessie," Shirley said, rubbing the back of the hand of the woman who used to be their Mother Superior.

"Hershey bars," Roberta said, rustling the bag in her hand. "Cheetos."

Tessie came to. Looked up at them through smeary lenses. "I forgot you were coming," she said, and pulled a tissue from the pocket of her blouse and wiped her lips.

"You look thirsty," Shirley said.

"And you look like shit," Tessie said. "Could you be any thinner?" Out of the corner of her eye, Roberta saw the nurse behind the desk look up for a second from the papers in front of her.

"I always wanted to be skinny" Shirley said, turning sideways to show off her flat stomach.

"Let's go out into the garden," Roberta said.

"It'll be too cold out there," Tessie said.

"We brought some warmth with us," Roberta said, lifting the thermos out of the food bag and handing it to Tessie.

"I'll get your jacket," Shirley said, "and a blanket."

Outside, Roberta and Shirley sat on the cement bench surrounding the statue of St. Joseph. Tessie faced them, the sun on her back, a blanket draped over her head and shoulders.

"You look like you have on the old habit," Shirley said.

"That bastard John the XXIII," Mother Theresa said, "he ruined everything."

"You sure have learned how to swear," Roberta said, as she set up a little bar on the seat next to her. The cold from the cement seeped into her cheeks as she made three gin and tonics. Shirley buttoned up her jacket and put on her gloves.

Tessie stretched her trembling hand out from beneath the blanket. Roberta handed her a drink. "You, Mother Theresa are shaking like an old wino."

"And I suppose you, Michaela, are still drinking like a fish."

Despite the jab, Roberta was pleased that Mother Theresa had called her Michaela.

ON THE WAY HOME, Shirley rode in the front seat. She held her jacket up to her neck, leaned forward into the heater. "I think this might be my last trip up here."

"Why do you need to see her, anyway?" Roberta asked. "She said you looked like shit."

"It's true I'm sure."

"And she didn't even say thank you."

"I'm not going to be around much longer."

"Oh, don't talk like that." Roberta kept her eyes straight ahead. Drove.

"What are you going to do," Shirley asked, "when I'm gone?"

"I'm going to be a semi driver," Roberta said, and sped up and pulled out around an old couple riding low in a Taurus.

"A semi driver?" Shirley leaned back into the seat and laughed. "You can't parallel park."

"I can learn," Roberta said. "Besides, when was the last time you saw someone parallel parking a semi."

"No really," Shirley said, "what are you going to do?" She tipped the seat back.

"Probably drink more," Roberta said. They had had this conversation before. Shirley wanted her to go to AA. Go back to the church. "For sure not visit Tessie the Terrible."

BY THE END OF JULY, Shirley was gone. For three days after the funeral, Roberta sat in the recliner and listened to Shirley's nieces empty out her apartment. They kept coming over and asking her did she want this or that and always she said no. When she heard the new people moving in, it was too much to bear and she went for a ride, past the old school, past the new school, onto the highway. Realized that the car was taking her to see Mother Theresa. At the Citgo Station she bought the ritual food.

"Are you drinking more?" the old woman asked.

The cement bench was warm today.

"I promised her I wouldn't," Roberta said. Around the garden, the women were parked in their wheel chairs in groups under the shade trees. An aide in a flowered smock wheeled a woman past them onto the grass. "Where's my cat?" the woman yelled over and over. "Where's my cat?"

"Your cat's dead," Tessie said, quietly.

Roberta laughed.

"What are you going to do?" Tessie asked, as she slipped the last Cheeto between her yellow lips.

"I'm not sure," Roberta said. She picked up their mess and threw it into the trash can on the edge of the lawn.

"Why don't you change your name back to Michaela," Tessie said as Roberta wheeled her back toward the building.

"Why would I do that?" Roberta asked, not admitting to the old woman that the thought had crossed her mind.

"You're a Michaela," Tessie said.

"And you're a Mother Theresa," Roberta said.

"Where's my cat? Where's my cat?" followed them through the door.

"How do you stand it here," Roberta asked in the

privacy of the elevator.

"Drugs," Mother Theresa said. They laughed.

The door opened. Roberta pushed her back to her place in the circle around the nurses' station.

"Will you be back, Michaela?" she asked.

"I think I will," Roberta said.

"Good. Bring a bigger bag of Cheetos next time," the old woman said and closed her eyes, "and more gin."

ON THE RIDE HOME, Roberta talked to herself. "Michaela, how are you feeling today? Michaela, are you hungry? Should we stop for lunch? Michaela..." It didn't seem to work.

At home, she sat in the recliner, swallowed the last of the drink in her hand, and listened to the new neighbors' TV. Just for tonight she would allow herself another drink, she decided. Just one more.

CAROL WOBIG

12   The Smell of Lilacs

M oira's paper sat white and crisp on the green blotter of my desk, waiting to be read. Early in the year, she'd stayed after class one day and asked me to tutor her in writing. Her parents would pay, she said. They wanted her to be the first in her family to go to college. I was thrilled to have an interested student, and said of course her parents didn't need to pay extra. It was my job. This was what I'd thought teaching would be when years ago I sat in the superintendent's office signing my first contract: a willing student, an admired teacher.

I gave Moira's essay an A+, recorded it in one of the last columns in my grade book and went home and busied myself with a cleaning project: the stove today. I pulled it out from the wall, set the burner bibs in a pan of ammonia in the sink.

While they soaked, I mixed myself a gin and tonic, and worked on my lesson plans until it was time to scrub away at the stove's already sparkling surface. With the second gin and tonic—I never allowed myself a third—I worked on my writing, a habit, along with the gin and tonics, that I kept to myself.

THE NEXT MORNING there was a note in my mail slot asking me to see the principal. What extra project did he want me to take on this late in the year? I knocked on his open door.

"Susan," Mr. Gerhart said. "Come in." He closed the door.

I sat down on the battered leather couch next to his desk, aggravated as always that he called me Susan instead of Miss Wilson, and aggravated with myself that I didn't have the courage to correct him. I held my lesson plan book in my lap, prepared to say that I had a full schedule for next year, couldn't take on any more work.

Mr. Gerhart sat down at his desk. He leaned back in his chair. It squeaked under his weight. He looked up at the ceiling, dragged his fingers through the few hairs still on his head. This must be a big favor. He made eye contact, finally, and I raised my eyebrows to him.

"Lenny gave this to me this morning," he said and

slid a fresh manila folder across the desk in my direction.

Lenny? Over the years, I'd had many run-ins with him about his slovenly cleaning of my room. I leaned forward and picked up the folder. Inside was a single piece of notebook paper that had been crumpled up and then smoothed out. I recognized Moira's handwriting. In a note to her boyfriend, she accused me of being in love with her, of squeezing her shoulder, of letting my hand linger too long. Then, the last line: "Do you think she's a L?"

"This is ridiculous," I said. My hand trembled as I slid it back at him.

"I didn't think there was anything to it," he said and caught the folder before it landed on the floor. "But you know I have to follow up on these things. I'll get back to you."

I nodded at his smiling face, left the room, and walked down the hall to the teachers' lounge, careful with each step to make sure I was placing my feet on solid ground.

In the lounge, smoke engulfed me. Matt, a science teacher, and Ethel, freshman English, sat across from each other at the long table, a stack of papers in front of them. They looked up at me and smiled, said hello. I took the mug with my initials on it off the rack on the wall, pressed the handle on the coffee urn, watched it fill my cup, pushing bits of dust up to the top.

"Some kids get it," Ethel said and wrote a note in red pencil on top of the page she was grading, "and some just don't."

The kids loved Ethel. Every year at graduation some senior said in a shaky voice how much they would miss her. I wished that she was a better teacher and wished I was more like her and my sister Rosalie. I knew I was cold and rigid, too rigid. No student ever said they would miss me.

"You okay?" Ethel asked. "You look kind of pale."

"Just tired," I said. And terrified — terrified that Moira's accusation would get around the school. I went to my classroom. It was a Wednesday. At the end of the day, Moira stayed after as usual.

"So, Moira," I said and ran my fingers over the uneven edge of the stack of essays on my desk. She didn't look up at me. Within the frame of her long black hair, I saw that her cheeks were on fire.

"You may go," I said. "The tutoring sessions are over."

She scooped up her books and fled, knocking the desk askew.

I corrected the essays in front of me, fighting again and again to keep the words from blurring.

Just as I finished, Lenny came into the room pushing a trash can ahead of himself, a mop in his right hand. His pants rested in a pile on the top of his work boots.

"Oh, excuse me," he said.

"Come in," I said, and placed the essays in the middle drawer of my desk and locked it. I stood and erased the next day's assignment off the board. "How long have you worked here?"

"The same as you, I think," he said, starting to move the first row of desks against the wall.

"And how long have you been monitoring my wastebasket?" I turned and dusted the chalk from my fingers.

"What're you talking about?" He pushed the last desk against the wall with too much force.

"You know what I'm talking about."

"Oh that," he said. "Just doing my job." He pushed the mop to the back of the room and turned. "Like you leaving me all those notes. Lenny do this. Lenny do that." He kept walking toward me and didn't stop until the blue fringe of the mop was almost on top of the toes of my pumps. "Oops, sorry," he said and backed up. "Just doing my job."

We glared at each other until he turned and shoved another row of desks against the wall. On shaky legs, I grabbed my purse and briefcase and walked out of the room.

I wanted to catch Mr. Gerhart before he left for the day. He was still in his office, on the phone, and motioned me to come in. I closed the door and sat in one of the chairs in front of his desk reserved for errant students and unhappy parents. He was confirming a golf date.

"I talked to Moira," he said after he hung up the phone.

His everyday tone of voice reassured me.

"The kids were teasing her," he said, looking at me now and then as he moved around the room getting ready to leave. He locked the black file in the corner of the room. "They were calling her teacher's pet, the usual. I explained to her that this was a serious accusation," he continued, and picked his briefcase up from the floor, set it in his chair and snapped the clasp shut. "She said she was sorry, that she didn't mean to get you into trouble. That you hadn't touched her."

I felt my face redden at the scene he'd just described: my principal asking my student if I'd touched her inappropriately. "And what will you do with the note?" I forced myself to ask and followed him out of the room.

"I'll check with the superintendent," he said and locked the door. "But don't worry about it." He faced me now, our briefcases hanging at our sides. "I'll explain to him what happened. It's not a big deal."

I nodded. Not a big deal to him, maybe.

"I have to run," he said, and hurried away from me.

I felt sick at the thought of the note sitting in his desk drawer waiting to be discussed with Mr. Randolph.

In the parking lot, I jammed the key into the ignition and sat in the idling car, the solidity of the brick wall of the school in front of me a temptation, but then remembered that I had promised to babysit for Rosalie's kids.

"Aunt Susie," Gretchen yelled, running out to the curb to greet me. I took my niece's sticky hand and walked up to my sister's open garage, a clutter of bikes and trikes and balls. Cardboard boxes, unpacked from the last move, leaned at odd angles along the back wall.

Rosalie came out the side door, her hair a new shade of red, her make-up freshly done and coordinated with the red hair.

"Thanks, Sis," she said digging in her purse for her keys. "I'll be back in an hour or two." She was going on her first date since her divorce. "The boys are eating," she yelled out the car window as she backed out of the driveway.

Al Jr. and Billie sat in front of the TV, a pizza in a box on the floor between them. Gretchen picked up a piece for herself and came back to the kitchen. I lifted her up into a chair and cleaned the kitchen while the children ate.

"Let's go outside," I said when they'd finished, and

reached in front of the boys and turned off the TV. They didn't protest, knew not to challenge me.

I sat in a lawn chair just inside the garage. The kids rode their bikes up and down the sidewalk. Gretchen had a pink bike with training wheels, and waved to me when she turned around at the bottom of the driveway. She would be like her mother. She would not be like me, a person with a hole in her center where nothing human caught. I could not face my classes the next day.

It was almost dark and a mosquito was buzzing around my head. I called the children in, got them ready for bed, and settled them in the living room. When I heard my sister's car in the driveway, I picked up my purse and left before she had time to tell me about her date.

At home, I poured the last of my bottles of gin down the drain, went through the day's mail and wrote out checks for the bills. I set my will, checkbook, and insurance policies out on the desk.

All my writing, pages and pages, the first years in spiral notebooks, the rest on typing paper in expandable folders, I tore into pieces and shuffled into black garbage bags. I carried the bags out to the garage, loaded them into my car, three heavy bags, then went back in and walked around the house one more time. I smoothed the bedspread, straightened the towels in the bathroom, brushed a hair off the sink and left the doors unlocked. Rosalie would have lost the keys I'd given her years ago.

I was relieved to be the only car on the two-lane road to the dump, a road lined with oak trees, their trunks as wide as the front end of my car. I turned into the empty parking lot. Heavy chains hung through the iron gates of the fence that surrounded the pit, a padlock in place. I got out of the car, opened the trunk, and threw the bags one by one over the fence. The last one burst open when it landed on top of a rusty engine.

White scraps of paper flew into the darkness. The smell of rotting food came to me in the humid night, and the smell of lilacs.

The branches of the bush, laden with purple cones, hung over the fence into the parking lot. A row of lilac bushes had lined the edge of my grandma's backyard. In the spring, she picked the blooms and set bouquets on every flat surface in the house.

My folks made fun of her, for her obsession with the lilacs and her other eccentricities. She was a Christian Scientist, a vegetarian, and gardened in her dead husband's overalls. They said the lilacs made her place smell like a funeral parlor, but I loved it and told her so. Some of us are just different, she would say to me when I helped her refill the vases. Some of us are just different. Then she would pull me to her soft chest and kiss the top of my head. I did love lilacs and had loved my grandma.

And I did love my gin and tonics, just two. I looked at my watch. If I hurried, I could get to the liquor store before it closed.

13 SPIC AND SPAN

I heard the crunch of tires on the gravel in the driveway, a last little rev of the engine.

"Kitty?"

"Out here."

Jack came around to the backyard, smiling. Maybe it would be a good night. He carried papers in his right hand. Maybe he'd bought the new refrigerator I wanted. No, a refrigerator wouldn't have brought a smile to his face.

"Daddy, Daddy," Peggy yelled from the swings. "Come push us."

He handed the papers to me and walked toward the girls. I was on my knees at the base of tree ten, trimming. I wanted to finish the yard work before supper, but set down the clippers and flattened the packet of papers on my thigh. I read the heading on the first page, looked up at him, looked back at the paper. Did I understand this? I stood up and walked toward the swings.

He kept pushing the girls and raised his eyebrows to me, a smile still on his face. "What do you think?"

I sat down on the edge of the sandbox, raised my eyebrows to him, no smile on my face.

"Push us higher," Marie said, and pumped her chubby legs toward the sky.

The girls' long hair, auburn like their dad's, flew out behind them.

"I drove up and looked at it today," he said, still smiling.

I nodded, kept my eyes on the papers. While I was home today, cleaning, cooking, refereeing fight after fight between the girls, he was off—without a word of warning to me—turning my life upside down. He'd made an offer on a restaurant. In a town I'd never heard of, couldn't even pronounce.

"Finish your clipping," he said and walked past me with a squealing daughter riding along on each of his shoes. "I'll get supper on the table."

"How far away is this town?" I called to his back.

"Two hours." He didn't stop or turn around.

Who did he think he was to just drop this on me? I got back to work. Hollow acorn caps dug into my knees. My wrist and fingers ached. At tree thirteen, the last one, I sat back, wiped away my tears on the tail of my shirt. The 5:47 from Cedar Junction swayed along the track toward Milwaukee. My cousin, in the back door of the caboose, waved to me. I waved back long after he would have been able to see me. I knew Jack wanted his own restaurant, but here, not two hours away from the only place I'd ever known, from the only people I'd ever known.

"Supper's on," he called through the kitchen window.

I thought I felt a cramp in my belly when I stood up, hoped I felt a cramp. My period was a week late. Until tonight I'd been excited about the possibility of another child, but hadn't told anyone.

"We're going to go to a new school," Peggy said when I came into the kitchen. Jack and the girls were sitting at the table.

"And live in a new house," Marie said.

"It's not for sure, yet, girls." I stood at the sink and let hot water run through my fingers.

"It is for sure. I made an offer." Jack reached over and cut up Marie's meat. "Bud's coming to list the house tomorrow night."

"So soon?"

"Yes, we have to act on it. The owner of the restaurant has another offer."

I sat down at the table, pushed my plate aside.

"Are you sick, Mommy?" Peggy asked.

"No, she's not sick," Jack said. "She's just excited about moving to a new place." He kept his eyes on his plate.

"We are, too," Peggy said.

"You'll have the house spic and span when Bud comes?" he asked.

"It's always spic and span, in case you haven't noticed."

"What did you say?" His loaded fork hovered before his mouth.

"Nothing," I said. "Eat your supper."

"Please don't fight me on this," he said. "You know I want to have my own place."

"I know it's your dream, and I want you to be happy, but—"

Marie tipped over her milk.

"Oh, shit." I grabbed a handful of napkins from the holder in the center of the table and sopped up the milk.

"You shouldn't swear in front of the girls," he said.

"Sorry," I said and threw the wad of napkins in the trash. I hated him. A man that an hour ago I would have said I loved, I hated.

"Will you push us on the swings again, Daddy?" Peggy asked. They trooped outside.

I cleared the table and tried to remember the last time Jack had given the girls this much attention.

The phone rang.

"You're not going to do this," Alma said after I told her what was going on. Alma, my older sister, a rock, a bossy rock. "You are not going to do this."

"I could just wring his neck. How could he do this to me?"

"You never should have married him. I tried to tell you."

"You did?" I couldn't remember anyone saying anything negative about him. "What did you say?"

"That he's an arrogant SOB. You told me I didn't know him like you did."

"Are you sure?" I heard his steps on the porch. "Gotta go."

He sat down at the table and looked over the contract and pictures. "We'll have our name painted on the front right away: Vogel's Restaurant." He ran his finger over one of the pictures.

I sat down across from him, picked at a piece of dried food on the edge of the table, heard the girls fighting in the driveway. "Maybe you should call it Jack's Place," I said to the top of his head.

"No, I think Vogel's is better." He kept reading the contract.

"I thought you were happy with your promotion."

"I was, but I can't stand working for Bendt anymore. He treats me just like my dad did. Nothing's ever right.

He's on my back all day long. Stop that fighting," he yelled toward the back door.

Silence, until the phone rang again.

"That's probably your other wonderful sister," he said and headed toward the basement.

"He's hell bent on doing this," I said. Alma, of course, had called Lillian.

"Let me talk to him," she said. Lillian was a wisp, but a fighter.

"No, no. That'll just make things worse. You know how he is."

"So what are you going to do?"

I arched my back to ease the kinks from the yard work. "I have until tomorrow night. Bud is coming to list the house after supper. I'm going to talk to Father Nowak. Can you take me up there in the morning? "

"I can. But what will he do for you?"

"Maybe he'll talk to Jack, talk some sense into his head."

"Good luck."

IN THE MORNING, I stood at the screen door of the rectory, ran my finger around the metal edge of the doorbell. Father Nowak was new to the parish. If only Father Kopecki was still here. I turned to leave, but stopped when I saw Melba walking across the lawn from the church.

"Are you here for the meeting?" She grasped the porch railing and pulled her thick body up the steps. "There's a coffee cake in the oven."

"It smells delicious," I said, "but I won't be able to make it to the meeting. Is Father in? I need to talk to him."

"Yes, he's here."

I followed Melba down the hallway.

"I'll let him know you're waiting."

In his freshly painted office, leather chairs flanked a maple desk, its surface bare except for a slab of glass and a statue of the Sacred Heart. An oil painting hung on each wall: one of the Archangel Michael, one of Saint Joseph, one of the Blessed Virgin—that was above the chair I sat in—and the fourth, The Last Supper. The pictures of the parishioners that had covered the walls of Father Kopecki's office had disappeared.

Father Nowak came into the room. I stood up. My pocketbook fell to the floor. With a hot face, I picked it up and sat down.

"How can I help you, Mrs. Vogel?" he asked after he settled himself behind the desk.

I collapsed my story into four sentences.

My husband was making us move. I didn't want to go. He was using our girls to coerce me. He sold our house without asking.

With a manicured nail, Father reached up and pulled

the edge of his Roman collar away from his substantial neck, tipped back in his chair, raised his eyes to the Blessed Virgin floating above my head, looked back at me. "And what would you like me to do?"

"Please, talk to him. Ask him to reconsider."

"You can't talk to him?" A phone rang in the distance. He glanced out the doorway, readjusted his collar again.

"He gets angry," I said and didn't add that I was afraid of his temper, and tried not to rile him.

"Well, Mrs. Vogel, you did take the vows. Your job as the wife is to obey your husband. That's what marriage is all about."

"But—"

Melba appeared at the door. "Phone call, Father," she said.

"No buts." He stood up. "You're married. Pray to the Blessed Virgin for strength, Mrs... sorry, Mrs...?"

"Vogel," I said, "Kitty Vogel."

"Mrs. Vogel," he said, "and I'll pray for you. It'll all work out." He left the room.

I passed Roberta and Rosie Miller and Marion in the hallway, each carrying a baking dish with pot holders.

"My sister's waiting for me," I said to their questioning looks and let the screen door slap shut behind me. I hurried uptown until I turned my ankle on the root of one of the elm trees shading the sidewalk and had to slow down. I was sweating. Moisture dampened my slip and garter belt, ran down my inner thighs. Was that blood I felt between my legs, or only sweat?

At the drugstore I limped into the rest room and peed: no blood. On the way back to the counter, I stopped and looked at the women's section, at a row of small jars that held one hundred tiny pills guaranteed to start your period. I picked one up and then set it back on the shelf. Would the Blessed Virgin have considered what I was considering? Probably not. But she wasn't married to Jack.

"How'd it go?" Lillian asked and slid what was left of her Coke over to me when I sat down next to her at the counter. "Why are you limping?"

"I turned my ankle." I reached down and took off my heels. "Father was no help. Told me to be a good wife. Obey."

"Priests have to stick to the party line," Lillian said and ordered each of us a hot fudge sundae.

"A sundae? It's nine o'clock in the morning," I said.

"So? We need a treat."

"I can't leave you," I said and hugged her, didn't let myself cry.

"Come and live with me," she said.

"Thanks," I said. "Alma gave me the same offer."

"You don't want to live with her?"

We laughed. We loved Alma, but she had five kids

of her own and lived on a farm that was in worse shape than the one we'd grown up on.

We ate our sundaes, careful to scrape every trace of chocolate and ice cream out of the bottom of the dish. Lillian set money on the damp check sitting between us.

Money. How would I support three, maybe four of us?

"Now what?" Lillian asked.

"I want to talk to Dad. Do you have time to take me out there?"

"Let's go," she said. "I have to be to work at one."

Once we were on the road, I stripped off my hose and garter belt, hesitated, and then threw them both out the window.

"Who are you?" Lillian asked and turned on to the road to the farm.

"I'm not sure anymore," I said, and punched her in the arm.

"Hey, watch it," she said and punched me back.

Up ahead, Dad was hunched over the steering wheel of the tractor, his head turned toward the mower cutting down the roadside weeds. He would help me, I didn't know how, but he would help me.

"Let me out here," I said. "I'll meet you up at the house." Dad let the tractor sputter to a stop. I pulled myself up next to him and sat on the hot fender. He unscrewed the lid of the fruit jar at his feet and offered me a drink of water and had a swig himself.

My face crumpled when I told him what was happening, though he probably already knew from Alma. He handed me his handkerchief and then rolled a cigarette, movements I'd seen him make so often: slide a paper from the packet, sprinkle tobacco from the pouch, roll a tight cylinder, lick the edge. He offered the first one to me, rolled one for himself. Sulfur lingered between us for a moment.

"Will you talk to him?"

He took a drag off his cigarette, lifted the straw hat from his head and smoothed back his damp hair, snuck a quick look at me, then scratched a spot behind his ear with his knobby fingers.

"He's a good man, Kitty, takes good care of you and the girls. Got the water into the house for us. I never could have done that myself."

"You won't talk to him?"

"I don't think I should interfere. Women go where the men go." He pulled on his work gloves, started up the tractor. "That's how it's always been. Once you're married, that's it." He smiled at me, reached over and squeezed my shoulder. "It'll all work out. Don't worry."

I stood up, pulled my dress away from my sweaty behind, and jumped down onto the sharp tips of the mowed weeds. As he drove away, the Queen Anne's lace fell in an even row behind the mower blades. I walked through the ditch and wedged an opening in the barbwire fence lining the cornfield, maneuvered myself through the hole, but managed to scrape my ankle on a barb. Why had I married Jack, I asked myself as I walked up the hill toward the house. I wasn't sure any more. At the time, he was a catch. Handsome, a city boy, made good money, bought me a house. We joked about it sometimes, that I'd married him to get off the farm.

At the top of the hill, I felt what I thought was a cramp. It stopped.

Lillian and Mom sat at the table in the kitchen having coffee. I collapsed onto a chair.

"Your ankle," Mom said. "Put it up here."

"It's just a scratch," I said.

"Lillian, get me a wet cloth would you? And the iodine." She dabbed at the blood on my ankle until it was clean.

I winced.

"I hate to say it, but you'll have to move," she said and lowered my leg to the floor.

I winced again.

"Once you're married, that's it."

It was what I expected from her.

"Did you ever think about leaving Dad?" Lillian asked.

Mom laughed. "I thought about it every day when you kids were little. I wanted to leave you all behind. But it got better."

"I have to pee," I said. That she'd even thought about leaving us was news to me. I went out the back door of the kitchen to the outhouse. A slant of sunlight through the cracks in the door highlighted my still pristine underwear. I was pregnant. I sat with my head in my hands until the rank smell of the outhouse turned my stomach and I lost my sundae in the hole next to me. I wiped my mouth on the hem of my dress and swung the door open for some fresh air.

"We have to get going," Lillian called from the back door of the kitchen.

AFTER SUPPER THAT NIGHT, Bud showed up as planned. I waited in the kitchen while he and Jack invaded my house with a clipboard and measuring tape. I stopped myself from making a pot of coffee, from setting the last two pieces of rhubarb pie on the table.

"I need you to sign these forms," Bud said to Jack when they walked back into the kitchen. "You too, Kitty."

"You didn't make any coffee?" Jack asked.

"It's kind of late. You'll be up all night," I said.

"I'll probably be up all night, one way or the other. I'm so excited. I almost told old man Bendt to shove it today." The men laughed.

"I need to check on the girls," I said and went outside. Peggy and Marie ran around the yard trying to capture the fireflies pulsing in the twilight. I stood next to tree number ten and ran my fingers up and down the crevices of its bark.

"Kitty," Jack yelled out the back door. "We need you to sign the papers."

I didn't move. I heard the back door open and close. Jack and Bud walked up next to me.

"We need you to sign these," Bud said and tried to hand the papers to me.

"Not tonight," I said.

"It's all set," Jack said.

"It's not all set," I said. "We have to talk."

"But—"

"No, Jack. We have to talk." I turned and walked back into the house.

14 FAULTLINES

The bolt turned with a heavy click, and the door of Pete's office swung open. The scent of his choice of pipe tobacco for the last twenty years, Captain Black Gold, knocked the breath out of Molly. She opened the window, steadied herself with the smell of cut grass rising from her neighbor's yard, walked back to her husband's desk. Sean wanted to take it to college with him next week.

"It's your fault," her son had shouted at her last night after a week of not talking to her. He sat at the kitchen table and wept. "Our life is over."

Molly wished she could say it wasn't her fault, that their life wasn't over, but she couldn't.

Pete's calendar lay open next to the phone. Before he died, she'd snuck in here now and again and flipped through the pages looking for signs of the affair she thought he might be having. She never found anything. It had taken her six weeks to enter this room again. Today, she saw black slashes through appointments scheduled after his death. So, it was planned. Until that moment, she'd kidded herself into thinking that he might have done it on impulse. That just before he lost consciousness, he might have regretted his decision with a last thought of her or Meghan or Sean, or Rusty.

Not so.

She closed the calendar and dropped it into a garbage bag but had to go back to the window for some air when she saw the bite marks on the stem of his favorite pipe. It lay in the ashtray Meghan — Meggie — had made for him at Girl Scouts Camp. Poor Meggie, Molly's constant companion now, though she had managed a sleepover at Lisa's last night.

Everything but the ashtray went into the bag: stapler and staples, rubber bands and paper clips, a stack of unused notebooks lying in the top drawer. The bottom drawer was locked. Now what?

She could pull it out far enough to pry it open and inserted a plastic ruler into the gap. It bent and snapped in two. A chip flew up and bounced off her forehead.

"Damn you, Pete." She kicked the desk. Her big toe throbbed.

She needed a heavy screwdriver but would have to

go into the garage to get one. Couldn't do that. She limped over to Leonard's yard.

"Can I borrow a screwdriver?" she yelled over the noise of his new riding mower, a concession to his age he'd told her. At the moment, she felt he was her only friend. She had to go back to work soon, knew the other teachers would be kind, but knew what they would be thinking, what she would have been thinking if this had happened to one of them. It was somehow her fault.

Leonard putted up to his garage. She followed. He turned off the motor.

"You're a sight," he said.

His idea of humor.

She looked down and saw the stains on her t-shirt, the dirt on the knees of her sweat pants. "I am a mess." Before—everything was before—she'd been meticulous about her grooming. For a time, she thought that she might be in competition with the thirty-year-old beauty new to Pete's department at the university. After supper one night, after a second glass of wine, she'd asked him if something was bothering him.

"No. Why would you ask that," he'd said and poured himself a third glass of wine.

"You're so crabby for one thing."

"Sorry," he said and kissed her on the cheek. "Just work. Which I should finish up before I'm too tired to think." He went to his office.

She should have pursued it, should have made him talk to her.

"Need help?" Leonard asked.

"No, I think I can do it, but thanks." She wanted to be alone when she unlocked the drawer and uncovered—what?

More notebooks. A stack of 8½" by 11" spirals, all black, all with a white label on the cover: Molly, Meghan, Sean, Rusty. A notebook for the dog? She almost laughed. This was the Pete she knew.

And a notebook for someone named Travis. Not Sharon, or Michelle, or Victoria, the name Molly had given to Pete's mistress after visiting the lingerie store and wasting money on a black teddy. Travis?

Don't stop and read them now, she told herself and slid the notebooks back into the drawer. She had to finish cleaning. The realtor. She had to have the house ready for Jean Anne.

She sprayed furniture polish on a cloth and dusted. Rusty wandered into the office and sniffed his way around the room and then settled into the nook under the desk.

Travis.

Who was Travis?

Travis. Probably a student. Pete was always heading out the door with his laptop over his shoulder to mentor someone, one of his behaviors that had brought suspicions to her mind. It's part of my job he would say when she suggested that his own children needed his time. But a whole notebook for a student?

She dusted the computer. What about an e-mail address for Travis? She didn't know Pete's password but was sure Sean could find it for her. No, she didn't want to get him involved in whatever this was.

The doorbell rang. Leonard, red-faced and sweating.

"Did the screwdriver work?"

"It did. How about a break from mowing?" She worried about Leonard, had made a batch of cupcakes last week for his eighty-second birthday.

After he helped her carry the bags from Pete's office out to the alley, they settled into lawn chairs in the back yard with iced tea. Rusty followed along.

"It's none of my business," she said, "but did you ever have an affair?"

Leonard looked at her and then reached down and stroked Rusty, who sat between them.

"You know, Pete asked me that same question a few months ago."

"He did?" So, he was thinking about leaving.

"Yeah. It was the day of that last big snow storm."

Molly remembered them following each other from one end of the block to the other with their snow blowers, taking care of the neighbors' sidewalks.

"I told him I had thought about it, years ago. We

were going through a bad patch then, but the kids were small. I couldn't leave them and he agreed with me."

"I just don't get it," Molly said and lifted her sweaty t-shirt from her chest, ran the iced tea glass across her forehead.

"Me neither," Leonard said and hoisted himself out of the lawn chair. "I better get back to work."

"Sorry," Molly said and followed him out to the back gate. "I didn't mean to make you uncomfortable."

"I'm not very good at this talk stuff," he said and laughed, "but I can fix this for you." He jiggled the latch on the gate.

"It would help me out," she said. "The realtor is coming tomorrow." She had to tell him.

"I figured it would come to that." He kept his head down, his eyes hidden beneath the brim of his Brewer's hat. "This just needs to be moved." He jiggled the lock again. "I'll fix it this afternoon and cut the grass, if you can get Sean out here to clean up." He turned and walked down the alley toward his back yard.

"Thanks, Leonard," she said. "Thanks."

He raised his hand in a wave but didn't turn around.

Molly decided to clean up the yard herself to avoid another fight with Sean. Rusty followed close behind as she picked up his piles. What had changed with Pete? Why did he decide to abandon his children—forever.

Rusty bumped into her leg.

"You poop too much," she said and scooped up another pile.

He looked up at her like she had just said I love you. She had to laugh. When she opened the garbage can and realized that she would be dropping the smelly bag in her hand on top of the ones holding the remains of Pete's office, she hesitated, but then dropped them in anyway and closed the lid.

Back in the office, she sat down on the floor next to the desk and pulled the notebooks out. The cleaning could wait. She'd start with hers. No, she'd start with Rusty's. A Polaroid of the dog and Sean was taped to the inside cover. They were the same height. On the first page, the dog's birth date. That was it.

The others were the same. Seemed Pete had planned to keep a notebook for each of them, but had lost interest. Hers stopped ten years ago with a sideways picture of her belly taken days before Meggie was born; Meggie's was empty; Sean's stopped after first grade.

She expected the same from Travis's, though his cover was soft and cracked. She hoped there was enough there to let her know who he was and why he was important enough to have a notebook. She opened it and leafed through page after page of dated entries. They seemed to be times and places for meetings, followed by pluses or minuses. How like Pete, the math professor.

The first entry:

4/10/1999. The Corner Café, 7 PM. + + + +!

The last:

3/18/2010. Starbuck's, 7 PM. - - - -

Three days later he was gone.

She went through the notebook again, closed it, and held it against her chest. The edge of a memory tried to surface, but she pushed it away. She had to find Travis. She took all the notebooks upstairs and hid them under her bed, the one she hadn't slept in since that night.

After a shower, she called Matt, Pete's colleague at the university, and asked him to meet her at the union.

"The only Travis I know," he said, "is Travis Anderson. He's in the office next to Pete's, sorry, what used to be his office." He raised his eyebrows to her. "Something I can help you with?"

"I don't think so," she said and stood up, "but thank you. I'd better do it myself."

After a good-bye hug, Molly walked over to the front door of the Math Building, stopped in the lobby and ran her finger down the glass of the directory. Room 433. Dr. Travis Anderson. She pushed the elevator button, but when the doors slid open, turned and left the building in the mass of students changing classes.

At home, she sat at Pete's computer and pulled up the university's website: Travis Anderson. Another math professor. His picture: unsmiling, black-rimmed glasses in place, black hair. She wrote his phone number on a Post-it Note, heard the back door open.

"Mom," Sean called out.

"In here," she answered and shut off the computer.

He stood in the doorway.

"You can come in," she said.

He stepped over the threshold. His bean pole body had taken on the shoulders of a man in the last months, a change she hadn't noticed until today. His dyed hair that she had noticed, jet black, hung over his collar in spikes. His jeans sagged. He walked past the fireplace, stood at the window for a moment, ran his fingers over a row of books in the bookcase. Rusty followed him.

"The desk is ready to go," she said. "I cleaned it out today."

"You cleaned it out?" Suddenly he was beside her pulling open the drawers and throwing them to the floor. Rusty ran out of the room.

"Stop," she said and pushed herself away from the desk. "Stop."

"I wanted his stuff, not just the damn desk. Where is it?"

"In the trash."

She followed him to the back door and watched him

dig through the garbage can. First the bag of dog poop hit the ground. Then Pete's bags. Sean sat on the grass and folded the tops open, removed each object like it was a relic. He let the paper clips run through his fingers, sniffed the bowl of Pete's pipe and slipped it into his shirt pocket along with his pens.

Why had she thrown out Pete's stuff before she checked with Sean? She was a person she didn't know, a person who could do nothing right. Nothing. Even cleaning out a desk. Maybe the world would be a better place without her, too.

No, that was crazy. No, the children needed her.

AFTER MIDNIGHT THAT NIGHT, when Meggie finally slept soundly on the couch, Molly called Travis's number and left a message. "Call me, please" was all she said and left her name and number. She tipped the recliner back and pulled the quilt up over her. The memory she'd been holding at arm's length all day took over.

They were in his dorm room, snuggling under the covers after making love.

"You make me feel like such a man," he'd said, and kissed her.

She'd taken it as a compliment that night but wondered about it the next morning as she walked to the other side of the campus to get her picture taken for the yearbook. She'd looked down at the engagement ring on her finger. They were graduating, getting married. You worry too much, that's what she said to herself, what he would have said to her. His comment didn't mean anything. You worry too much.

IN THE MORNING, Molly followed the realtor through the house as she made notes on her clipboard. When they got close to the garage, Molly pressed the door opener and stepped back. Leonard had gotten rid of the car for her, but the tools still hung on the pegboard, all within outlines.

"You know what happened here?"

Jean Anne made more notes. Molly had found Pete in the morning, grateful that he'd at least had the sense to do it while the children were at their grandmother's for a last weekend at the cottage before school started.

"I do," she said and stopped writing. "I'm—"

"Will it matter?" Molly took a step away from the realtor and crossed her arms over her chest.

"I don't think so," Jean Anne said. "It's a nice house. People overlook that kind of thing if the price is right."

"Make it right then," Molly said.

The phone in the kitchen rang. "I have to get that," she said, and hurried toward the front door.

"I'll get back to you with a price," Jean Anne said and left.

Inside, Molly listened as Travis left a phone number. Call anytime he said. She listened to it again and wrote the number down. His voice was low, sad, not unkind. She listened to the message one more time and then erased it.

She called him. They would meet at 7 PM, in his office.

No, not in his office she said. At the coffee shop.

MOLLY SAW HIM when she walked in the door. He sat at a corner table upstairs and didn't really wave but lifted his hand to her. He must have known who she was for years, and the children, from photos in Pete's office. She stopped and ordered a coffee, walked up the stairs.

Pouches and creases layered the face that was on the website. The curls were grey, the heavy black glasses remained.

"I found your notebook," she said and sat down across from him.

"My notebook?"

Molly reached into her purse and pulled it out, slid it toward him.

He paged through it from front to back, closed it, cupped his hands around his glasses.

She'd been a fool, such a fool. She didn't know what to say, just sat and stared at her husband's lover.

"It was my fault." He wiped his eyes with a napkin.

His fault?

"We'd been together for ten years and in a moment of anger, I gave him an ultimatum. You or me. I threatened to out him. That was our last meeting, here at this table."

"I thought it was my fault," she said.

"No. I'm to blame." He wiped his eyes again. "I was a fool. I thought he'd know that I loved him, that I wouldn't have outed him. I thought we'd make up again in a few days and things would go on as usual."

"Well, there seems to be enough pain to go around," Molly said, a quaver in her voice. She stood up, made it down the stairs, out the door.

At home, she didn't go into the house, but sat on the front porch. The leaves on the trees hung perfectly still in the last light of day. Through the screen door, she heard the TV and Meggie's laughter, then the click of Rusty's toenails and Sean's heavy footsteps coming toward the front door. Sean sat on the top step, his back to her. Rusty sat next to him.

"You know, what you said the other night was partly right," she said. "Our old life is over, but there's still time to build a new one."

"You really believe that?" Sean wrapped his arms around Rusty, pulled him close.

"I do," she said. "I'm sure." And she wished she could

say the same words to Pete, to Travis. "It won't be easy, but there's still time." She heard Meggie laughing at something on TV. "Let's go in," she said. "We have to take care of her and Rusty. And you."

"Okay," Sean said, "okay." He draped his arm over her shoulder as they walked back into the house. Rusty trotted behind them, happy as always.

There's still time, Molly told herself. There's still time.

15 TYING UP TO THE PIER

Rachel lives in town. She takes me shopping on Wednesdays, which I do appreciate. She's the youngest of my kids, and the bossiest. She has a list of things I should do: sell the cottage, move into town, fix my bunions, cut my hair. She doesn't like that I look like the old lady I am, my gray hair in a scrawny knot, my fat covered with polyester pants and flowered tops from Walmart.

She supervises me all day long when we shop. "Mom, do you see that curb? Mom, do you need to use the restroom? Mom, don't order that. It's full of fat."

I'm only seventy-eight, not a hundred and eight.

So, it's Wednesday and I have to put away the groceries, but first I need to get these loafers off. I only wear them when I go out with Rachel, and I do look with love on my old tennies when I walk in the door.

Wally cut holes in them to relieve the pressure on my bunions.

It is odd to come home to an empty house. Wally's coffee cup still sits on the counter with a spoon standing in it, a "Gone Fishing" note under its edge, the paper yellow and curled. It was his dream, this cottage. We moved out here for good when he retired. I love it, too, but yesterday I noticed that the front porch is leaning forward a bit. Maybe it needs to be propped up. What would that cost? And I can't really keep up with the outside work. The trees are starting to drop their leaves. Next will be the snow. What will I do about that?

Another problem. All summer, I've slept on a lawn chair out on the porch. Some nights I start out in the bedroom, but before long I'm out on the porch. It isn't death, that Wally died in the bed. I knew it was coming, and in the end found myself wanting it to come for his sake and mine. I've washed everything, aired it out for weeks, but still can't breathe when I lie down in there.

And my worst problem is the pictures. Not only did Rachel take dozens at every Christmas and birthday, but she fixed them in frames, brought them over and hung them on the walls and arranged them on every flat surface in the cottage. Even in the bathroom. Now I have to walk through the place like an old horse with blinders. They're attacking me. I could just take them down, but she'd have a fit.

Lots of the pictures are of Wally and his best buddy, Willy. I know, Wally and Willy, the teasing never stopped. Willy's tying up at the pier right now. He just threw a stringer of fish out of the boat and is hoisting himself up onto the pier.

I meet him at the fish table by the back door. "Nice catch."

"Got a couple of perch." He holds them up by the gills.

I sit on an overturned bucket, rest my back against the warm shingles. Scales fly up his arms and into the white hair fuzzing up over his undershirt.

"Just one'll do," I say, when he hands me four fillets.

"You know, Anita, sometimes I forget he's gone."

"Not me," I say. "I've got all of these damn pictures looking back at me day and night."

"Just take them down. I can do it for you." He wraps his fillets in newspapers and hoses down the table.

"It's not that simple." I sweep the fishy water out onto the grass.

"Rachel?"

"I'm afraid of her." I laugh, but it's the truth. "I'm afraid she'll think I've gone off the deep end and haul me off to the home."

"I'll stand up for you," Willy says, and buttons up his shirt.

"Thanks," I say. "We'll see what happens." I stand at the top of the stairs and watch him walk back down to the lake, the bundle of fish under his arm. He looks up and waves before he pulls away from the pier.

That night, the temperature drops. I wrap myself up in two of the kids' old sleeping bags, and add one of Wally's knit hats and a pair of gloves to my ensemble. Cold as it is, one last mosquito buzzes around my neck until I give up and let the damn thing bite me. I can't sleep anyway. The cottage. The leaves. The snow. The pictures. The cold. If I move the wrong way, the cold sneaks in and I have to readjust everything.

IN THE MORNING, warm in my cocoon, I listen to the radio I keep out here. A cold front is on the way. Now what? I really don't want to wake up under a blanket of frost. Wally died on May 12th, almost six months ago. I do know what Oprah's advice would be: I should kick myself in the butt and move on. The other day on her show she said that if you want something, you should imagine it first.

So, I get dressed and take my coffee down to the lake, sit on our old boat that's pulled up on the shore, close my eyes, and try to get my imagination in gear. The sun warms my face, the lake laps the shore, and next thing I know I fall asleep and dump the coffee into my lap.

"Hey, Anita!" Willy putters up to the pier, cuts the engine. "I need to talk to you."

I walk out on the pier. My wet pants slap against my thighs.

"I forgot to tell you yesterday," he says, after we have a good laugh about my pants, "I told Wally I'd take care of the yard for you, and the snow."

"Oh, yeah?" I fold my arms and look over toward the island so he doesn't see my eyes fill up. "That'll be great. I was worried." Wally, my sweet Wally, taking care of me from the other side.

"And I'll see if I can find somebody to brace up the porch before it snows," Willy adds. He reaches back and pulls the cord on the motor and backs away from the pier. "I'll get back to you."

"Thanks," I say. He guides his boat out to the middle of the lake and drops a line.

All that's left are the pictures. What would Wally want me do? He'd want me to be comfortable in the cottage he loved. Protect me from Rachel, I say to him, and walk back up the hill.

I carry all the pictures out to the kitchen table, open up frame after frame, and drop the photographs into plastic grocery bags. The frames I stack in a box for Rachel and wait for her daily death call. At 11:01

the phone rings. "I'm out shopping." she says. "Do you need anything?" "I do," I say. "A bucket of white paint." "What are you going to paint?"

"Oh, I'm losing you," I say and hang up. My people on *The Guiding Light* do that all the time, but it's a first for me. Feels good, until after lunch, when I hear tires on the gravel in the driveway.

"Let's sit out here." I try to steer Rachel toward the lawn chairs under the oak tree.

"I don't have time," she says and carries the paint into the house.

I sit out by the fish table. My heart pounds.

In no time, she flings herself out the back door and stands above me, the box of frames in her arms. "What are you doing? Have you gone crazy? All my work?" She drops the box at my feet and rushes off to her car and drives away.

I sit there for a few minutes and take deep breaths, calm down. Then I get back to work.

I pull the nails out of the walls, wipe away the dust and paint out the shadows of the frames, but still feel the pictures stalking me.

I clean up the brush and make one more trip down to the lake. With the bucket we used to bail out the boat, I fill the bags of photographs with sand and pebbles, tie them up, walk them out to the end of the pier, and sail them out into the lake as far as I can. After not much of a splash, they disappear. When my legs stop shaking, I drag myself back up the stairs and collapse onto the bed.

At 3:17 a.m. I wake up, reach my arm out and squeeze my hand between the mattress and box spring and pull out the one picture I saved. I set it up on the bedside table, roll over, toasty warm beneath our wedding quilt, and sleep.

CAROL WOBIG

16 OREOS

Jerry came out the front door of The Institute. There was something different about him today. The ring of keys that always hung from his belt loop was gone. He had a new haircut, had lost weight. Before I hoisted myself out of the car, I slipped the half-eaten package of cookies on my lap under the seat and dusted the crumbs off my chest.

"Well, Jerry, what's going on with you?"

"What?" He ran his hand through his new hairdo.

"What? You look like a new man. Are you in love? And what happened to your keys?"

"The locks are all electronic now," he said, "and the rest is none of your business." We laughed.

"You've been sitting here for a long time, Alice. Having trouble going in?"

"As usual," I said, and took the arm he offered

to me. We walked back toward The Institute like a couple, a fantasy I'd held onto when I was a teenager, a fantasy that helped me through the early years of visiting my mother here, and maybe could save me again. I'd never given up on him, knew from the grapevine that he'd gotten divorced.

Inside, I stopped at the receptionist's desk. "Is that music I hear?"

"You betcha." Jerry waltzed a few steps and laughed. "This is a classy place now."

"Nice," I said and signed in.

"Do you want me to walk you back?"

"No, thanks. I know the way." I walked a few steps and turned around. "Want to meet for a beer later?"

He stopped walking toward his office. Didn't answer or turn around.

"If you have time," I added.

"Sure, let's do that," he said.

"Frank's? 6:30?"

"Okay," he said and walked into his office.

"The Tennessee Waltz" drifted in and out of the blades of new ceiling fans in the hallway. I loved to waltz, took an imaginary step or two with Jerry but forced myself to keep moving toward the remodeled dayroom. My mother sat on a flowered couch, her head forward, her eyes on her work. A slant of sunlight from a skylight rested on the pink scalp beneath her white hair. Her hands, balanced on the pile of flesh that was her belly, poked a silver crochet hook in and out along the edge of a green potholder.

"Mother?" I touched her knee. "It's Alice. I've come to visit." She didn't look up. "Hazel?" I said loud and clear. She looked up. "The place sure looks beautiful," I said.

"It's warmer now and doesn't stink like it used to." She kept crocheting. In the early years, she'd almost finish a potholder and then unravel the stitches and start over, only wanting to work with the same soiled, rippling yarn. These days, she finished the potholders and they sold them in the gift shop.

"I want to show you something." I took a picture out of my purse.

Hazel kept her eyes on her work.

I moved the picture over under her eyes. "I fixed up Joe's room for you. I want you to come and live with me."

"What's wrong with Joe?" She stopped crocheting, looked straight ahead.

"Nothing, nothing, Mother. He's off to college in Madison."

She resumed her work, pushed the picture away. "You know I can't leave here."

"That was in the old days," I said. "You can do whatever you want to now."

"I need to stay here. I'm too old to change."

"Even for me?"

She didn't look at me, but stopped crocheting and stuffed her handiwork into a bag. "I'm sorry, but I just want to stay here. They said I should stay here." She reached for her cane and pulled herself up off the couch.

"They didn't say you should stay here," I said. "They said you could stay here. There's a difference."

"I know what you want." She turned and walked away from me.

I followed her down the hall to her room.

"I sent your brother to town on his bike for five pounds of flour, five lousy pounds—"

"It was an accident," I said and leaned my forehead against the door she'd just closed in my face. "It was an accident." The same words Dad had yelled at her over and over until the day she tried to kill herself.

I stood there until I heard her TV come on and then headed back to the lobby, the new pictures on the walls lost in a blur.

Jerry sat behind the receptionist's desk, doing a crossword. "Do you know a six-letter word for frustration?"

"Mother," I said. "She turned me down again." I showed him the picture.

"Nice," he said and handed it back to me. "But why don't you just give it up like your dad did? It's too much pain to deal with. I see it all the time."

"I can't," I said. "I know I should, but I just can't."

"Okay," he said and stood up. "You're the boss."

He escorted me out to the car, and I reminded him again to meet me for a beer. "6:30?"

"I'll be there," he said and closed the car door for me, tapped good-bye on the roof, and walked back into the building.

The prospect of meeting Jerry later, even though I'd invited him, lifted my spirits. I took a right onto County G, knowing it was a mistake, and headed toward Dad's farm. The Oreos on the seat next to me disappeared.

Over the next hill, I caught up with a school bus and waited behind it at stop after stop until it braked at the farm's driveway and unloaded Dale and Richard.

After I reminded the boys that I was their stepfather's older daughter, I gave them a ride up the gravel driveway. In front of the house, before I even turned the engine off, they jumped out of the car and raced over to the rope swing on the oak tree closest to the kitchen, the best swing, the one Albert and I used to fight over — before the accident. Everything was before.

A shiny black Dodge Dakota, "Hilldale Farm" spelled out in silver letters on the door, sat parked in front of what used to be the falling-down house. The roof was new, the white siding sparkled, rockers and hanging plants lined the porch.

"Come in," Lana said through the screen.

I hadn't been able to make myself go to Dad's wedding. Lana had even asked me to be a bridesmaid, and I felt like I should have been more understanding, should have been happy that Dad had finally thawed and found someone to be with. I'd even bought a new dress at Lane Bryant, but in the end stayed home and watched the Packers game. They lost.

"The house sure looks nice," I said.

"I fixed it up." She ran water into a coffee pot. "Had a ball. Your dad's so good to me and the boys. They just love him."

"Really?" I said.

"Oh yes. He's the father they never had." She plugged in the coffee pot.

"Well, getting rid of the fly-papers is a definite improvement," I said.

We laughed.

"I'll let him know you're here." She picked up a walkie-talkie from the butcher block island.

I took a chance and walked into the dining room. The vent in the ceiling to the upstairs bedrooms was still there. Once, with the promise of a Hershey bar, I got Albert to look up at me and I dumped a glass of water on his sweet face.

When I heard Dad's voice on the walkie-talkie I hurried back into the kitchen before memories could bring me to my knees on the new carpeting.

"I'm busy," came over the radio.

"Sorry," Lana turned to me. "He just works all the time."

"I should've called," I said, though I knew it wouldn't have made any difference. He hadn't talked to me since the wedding, except to holler into the phone one night that I was just like Mother, didn't want him to have any happiness in his life. I was just like my mother, but not in the way he thought.

"How about a cup of coffee?" Lana asked.

I looked at my watch. "Thanks, but I'll have to pass." I walked out the door, down the hill to the tan pole barn that dwarfed the crumbling foundation of the old one. Dad didn't want to see me. Fine. I wanted to see him. I stood in the doorway of the new building, lost for a moment in the smell of manure, the click and suck of the milking machines.

A worker saw me. "Ray!" he yelled.

Dad's head poked up above the back of a cow farther down the row. He said something to the man next to him and limped toward me. "I told you I'm busy."

I followed him outside. "What's wrong with your leg?"

"Goddamned cow kicked me." He sat down on a

bench next to the barn and massaged his knee.

"Did you go to the doctor?"

"No." He pulled a half-pint out of the pocket of his blue coveralls, took a swig. "I have my own medicine."

"You always did." I sat down next to him. My ample rear rested against his bony hip.

"And you're as fat as ever," he said, and lit up a Camel.

"Thanks," I said and moved away from him.

"Well," he said after a couple of drags on his cigarette, "I'm sure you didn't drive all the way out here to check up on my knee. If it has to do with your mother, just forget it. She made her choice years ago."

"It's not about Mother," I said and crunched the picture I'd pulled out of my purse into a wad and let it drop to the ground. "I drove up here to have you tell me I'm fat."

"Don't litter up my place," he said and took another swig of whiskey. "I can't talk anymore. I've got work to get done." He picked up the picture without looking at it, pressed it into the bucket of sand next to the door, and limped back into the barn.

I dragged myself up the hill to my car. A choice? Had she made a choice back then?

At the end of the driveway, I made the choice to throw my empty Oreo package onto Dad's perfectly mowed grass and turned back onto County G. Jerry was waiting, maybe just for me.

At Frank's, he sat at the end of the bar next to another man. They both wore pressed white shirts, jeans with a crease, shiny leather loafers, kind of dressed up for a little country bar that sat on a patch of dirt carved out of a cornfield.

"This is Tim," Jerry said.

I nodded to him, pulled myself up onto the barstool.

"You look like you could use a drink." Jerry ordered me a beer.

"Too much family." I tried to laugh. The bar had been sold since the last time I'd been there, but looked the same except for the posters, all of James Dean who slouched on the cracked mirror behind the dusty liquor bottles, slouched next to the Hamm's sign still pushing water over the dam, slouched on the door of the men's room.

"What's with all these posters?"

"Frank's has changed," Jerry said and gave me a sideways look.

I took a drink of beer, licked the foam off my upper lip. A young man dropped a handful of quarters into the juke box. "Unchained Melody," a song that always made me want to cry, filled the room. In the mirror in front of me, a couple moved out of the darkness of the back booth toward the dance floor, one a James Dean look-alike—and the other a James Dean look-a-like. It took me a minute to put it all together.

I turned to Jerry. He sat with his eyes glued to the beer in front of him, his hands wrapped around the glass.

I reached over and touched the back of his wrist with the tip of my index finger. "Let's go outside."

"Be back in a minute," he said to his friend.

We walked across the rutted parking lot, arm in arm again, silent as the stars just appearing in the blue of the fall sky, and sat on a picnic table.

"Hope you're not shocked," he said.

"No, just surprised." I laughed. "Okay, shocked. You sure had me fooled. I was in love with you for years." A cool breeze rustled the dried leaves on the stalks of corn that stood behind us like meddling neighbors. I pulled my sweater closer to my body.

"Sorry," he said. "I kind of knew that. I wanted to tell you the truth, but I only admitted it to myself when I met Tim."

I reached over and rubbed his back, swallowed, and pulled the wavering lines of the world back into place.

"I'm happy for you," I finally managed to say. And I was. His pain was probably over. "I'd better get going."

In my car, I rested my head on the steering wheel. Thirty-seven years of Jerry fantasies along with my mother fantasies emptied from my brain and left me hungry. I retrieved my emergency package of Oreos from the trunk and headed home.

CAROL WOBIG

17 SHOULDER TO SHOULDER

On the next Wednesday after practicing—she did love her teacher, Natalia, maybe ironing wasn't her only talent— Marge unzipped the garment bag holding her funeral dress, laid it out on the bed. Did people dress up to go to the airport? She put it back in the bag, the bag back in the closet. She took it out again. Yes. They do.

Looking at herself was a trial. She'd always been large, big-boned her mother had said, and now her skin, rippled and crinkled, hung from those bones. And the teeth. Always the teeth. There never had been the money for braces. Now there was life insurance money, but she should keep that for house repairs, if she didn't do herself in. No, she wasn't going to do herself in. Irene needed her, and Freddie was coming to visit. He'd called last night. She turned away from the mirror, switched to her patent-leather purse and dusted off her black flats. Better to be overdressed than under.

She'd thought about asking Melody to take her to the airport to pick up Freddie, but while her daughter was over her snit about not getting the piano, she and her brother didn't always get along. And Freddie didn't sound—she couldn't put her finger on it—just didn't sound like Freddie. Had he lost his job? Was he homeless?

At the airport—how'd she found it and parked without an accident she wasn't sure—Marge stood like an island amidst the rush of travelers laden with backpacks and rolling suitcases, all wearing jeans. She read the screen telling her where her son would arrive, but did not realize she couldn't go through security without a ticket. So she waited where the agent told her to and kept pressing the folds of the skirt close to her thighs to minimize her width. Why had she worn this dress? She felt like a float in a parade.

People hurried towards her up the ramp alone and in bunches, and after a long gap Freddie appeared. Ah, yes. Her son, looking older, tanned, thin, too thin. She waved to him, was surprised by the tears that threatened. He strode toward her and hugged her, a maneuver so unexpected that she stood there, engulfed in his arms like a statue. They weren't a hugging family.

A younger man stood to Freddie's left, smiling.

"This is my friend, Jeff," her son said.

"Nice to meet you," she said, and shook his extended hand. Did he need a ride, too? She wasn't running a taxi service.

"Jeff wants to see the Midwest," Freddie said. "I hope it's okay that I brought him along."

"Oh, sure. We have lots of room." How like her Freddie. To take in a stray, to not tell her. Was the roast in the crock pot enough for dinner?

He had driven home, much to her relief. She sat in the back seat, to give Jeff a better view. As she mentally inventoried the refrigerator for ingredients for side dishes to add to dinner, she worried about Freddie. His ears looked huge, stood out from the tight skin on his neck and jaw.

"Sure smells good," he said, as they walked up the back steps into the kitchen.

"I'm going upstairs to change," Marge said. "We'll eat in a minute." In the bedroom, she unzipped the dress, hung it up, pinned a note to it that said "Burial Dress."

Downstairs, the boys, funny how that phrase came to her mind, the boys were at the counter, their shoulders touching, making a salad. "How nice of you," she said. They stepped apart at the sound of her voice.

"What happened to the dining room table?" Freddie asked.

"I traded it for the piano. Your father—"

"Don't worry about him," Freddie said. "We'll eat in the kitchen. Do you have any wine?"

"No, sorry." Marge arranged the meat and vegetables, cooked to just the right tenderness, on a platter. "But check the bottom drawer of the desk."

Freddie returned with a half-full bottle of Jack Daniel's. "Why did he hide it?" he asked.

"It was a game we played," she said, "I didn't care. I think the bottle lasted for years."

"What a guy," he said. "What a guy."

Yes, what a guy and why weren't you here for the funeral Marge wanted to yell at him, but didn't. She wasn't a yeller. And why were your shoulders touching? And why are you so thin? "Did you meet on the plane?" she asked as the boys ate and helped themselves to seconds.

"This is a great dinner," Freddie said, his eyes on his plate.

She was happy to see him eat. A few strands of gray were visible in the wave of hair over his forehead. "Did you meet on the plane?" she asked again as she brought out the rhubarb pie she'd made from scratch.

"Oh, my favorite," Freddie said.

"I've never tasted rhubarb," Jeff said. He pursed his lips, wiped the edges of his black mustache.

"You got it all," Freddie said and they smiled at

each other and laughed.

They certainly liked each other.

"We didn't meet on the plane," Freddie said. "He grew up in California. You know how they are out there." They grinned at each other, again. "We've been friends for a long time."

So, he wasn't a stranger, to Freddie anyway, though he looked too young for them to have been friends for a long time. And he looked so healthy next to Freddie, thick black hair, pink cheeks, strong shoulders.

"Great meal," Jeff said. "Love the rhubarb."

Well, he couldn't be all bad.

"We'll clean up," Freddie said.

That was a first. "Okay," Marge said. "It's time for my program anyway."

The contestants spun the wheel, Vanna turned the letters, Marge fell asleep. When she woke up, the kitchen was clean, the house quiet. She should practice, she had a lesson tomorrow, but didn't think she could do it with the boys in the house. And where were they? She looked out the window over the sink.

They were sitting on the bench in the snow, shoulder to shoulder again, passing a pipe back and forth. A pipe? She stepped back and wiped her glasses on the dish towel hanging on the handle of the stove, hung it up, evened up the edges, took a deep breath and looked out the window again. They were sitting separately now, laughing at something. Not her dress, or her teeth, she hoped. She must have been seeing things. Just what she had said to Bud when he saw Freddie and the neighbor boy—what was his name? Alan. He practically lived with them, Alan—lying together on the bed in Freddie's room watching TV.

"What's going on here?" Bud had yelled. He was a yeller. "Are you a couple of fags?"

She never heard Freddie's answer, only the slam of his door after Alan came running down the stairs and out the back door without saying good-bye.

Bud stomped into the kitchen then, red-faced, his hands trembling. "I need a drink."

Calm down, Marge had told him and got him a beer from the fridge. "You're seeing things. They're just kids."

They'd never talked about it again, except to wonder as Freddie neared forty if he'd ever get married, if they'd ever have more grandchildren. Marge had her suspicions, but she kept them to herself and squelched them when they caught her off guard.

During the night, on one of her trips to the bathroom, she thought she heard quiet voices coming from the bedroom they'd chosen—it did have twin beds. Were they talking all night? Playing cards? And what was that smell? Were they smoking that pipe again? She hoped they didn't burn the house down.

Thurs. a.m.

Irene,

Sorry I didn't write yesterday. Too much going on. Freddie has come to visit. I'm nervous. There is a note on the table. They've gone for a walk uptown and want to talk to me when they get back.

Marge

She couldn't eat her oatmeal or focus on the crossword. Had Melody called Freddie and told him that she was losing it, needed to be in a home because she was taking piano lessons? Or just losing it? No, she wasn't losing it. She had driven to the airport. She did want to practice before they got back but first went upstairs, looked into the boys' bedroom to see if the beds were made. They were, though the blinds needed straightening. She walked into the room. Stopped. A cluster of orange pill bottles on the nightstand took her breath away. On wobbly knees, she turned, found her way down the stairs and sat at the piano, just sat there, her fingers on the cold keys. She had to practice. Yes. She had to practice. Practice, she told herself, practice. She took a deep breath, plunked away with trembling hands, the pills looming above her, and didn't hear the boys come in the back door. Suddenly, they were standing in the dining room, clapping for her.

"Great, Mom, great," Freddie said and hugged her shoulders.

"You caught me," she said, felt his bones against her back.

"We brought lunch," Jeff said and held up a bag from the new café downtown.

The lunch included food she hadn't eaten before, but she gave it a try, even the hummus that looked to her like something you wouldn't want to eat. What did they want to talk to her about? She hadn't forgotten about the note—or the pills. What about the pills? Dessert was key lime pie, she did like that, remembered the first time she'd eaten it on her honeymoon in Chicago and was relieved that Bud was gone now.

"Close your eyes," Freddie said, after the table was cleared.

Now what? Her heart pounded.

"Okay, open," Jeff said and handed her a bag from the Boston Store.

She pushed her chair away from the table and set the bag on her lap. "I love the Boston Store but don't go there much anymore. Or not at all."

"Open it," Freddie said.

They smiled at her like they had just come home from school with report cards with all A's. She hoped she liked whatever it was. Wrapped in tissue was a beautiful, yes, she had to say beautiful, blue dress. A suit really. But soft material, and flowy. She held the jacket up to her shoulders. "Looks like the right size," she said, "but it must have cost a lot. I don't really need anything like this."

"You will," Freddie said and handed her an envelope.

Inside was an airline ticket to San Diego.

"We want you to come to our wedding."

Marge looked from Freddie, to Jeff, and back to Freddie, whose arm rested on Jeff's shoulder. "You're getting married?"

"We are," Freddie said and kissed Jeff on the cheek.

"Well, I'll be," Marge said. "I'll be. And you're having a wedding?" She looked at the ticket in her hand.

"Of course. And we want you to be there."

"You do?"

"Yes. We do." They grinned at her.

"My family will be there," Jeff said.

A car pulled into the driveway. The back door opened. Melody.

Trouble.

"Like the outfit," Freddie said, and hugged his sister.

Melody was in a red phase: red hair that cost a fortune, matching red lipstick, dangling red and silver earrings atop a black leather jacket and tight jeans. Too tight for her age, Marge thought but didn't say.

Freddie introduced her to Jeff, and then they went out back for a smoke. Melody helped herself to the last piece of the rhubarb pie.

"What's in the bag," she asked, as Marge poured them a cup of coffee.

"A gift from the boys."

"The boys?" Melody looked out the window over the sink. "You know what they're doing out there, don't you?

"Smoking. Sharing a pipe. It does have an odd smell."

"You're a dinosaur," Melody said. "It's dope." She abandoned her pie and looked at the dress. "It's beautiful," she said and held it up to herself. "But way too big for me."

"Marijuana?"

"Yes, marijuana," Melody said." You don't really need this dress, do you?" She folded it up and put it back in the bag. "They should have given you the money."

"Is that legal?" Marge's heart was pounding again. She got up and looked out the back window.

"Sort of. Relax. You're so out of touch."

"I know, I know." Marge sat down at the table, cut into the tip of the last piece of key lime pie but couldn't eat it. May as well get this over with. She slid the envelope with the ticket across the table to Melody.

"San Diego? You're going to San Diego?"

"Maybe." Marge said. "Freddie's getting married."

"Wow. After all these years. Maybe I'll go with you. Who's the lucky girl?"

Marge couldn't take much more of this. "Jeff."

Melody froze, set her fork down. "Freddie is gay?"

Marge nodded.

"And he's still in our house?" Melody stood up and threw her pie plate into the sink.

"Of course," Marge said. "He's my son. Your brother. And don't throw my dishes around."

"I always knew there was something wrong with him. Dad did, too."

"There's nothing wrong with me," Freddie said, as he and Jeff walked into the kitchen.

Marge hadn't heard the backdoor open.

"You're the one with the problem," he said.

"The Church—"

"Oh, screw the Church."

"And screw you," Melody said, grabbing her purse and slamming the door on her way out.

"Wow," Jeff said. "Time for some wine." He opened the bottle on the counter.

Marge lowered her head into her hands, pressed her fingers into her eyes. "I need to think. I'm going to my office." She went down to the basement, sat on the bottom step. This was all her fault. She'd been a rotten mother. And Freddie was sick. Who knows what kind of hell he'd been through because she didn't face reality, because she was afraid of Bud, listened to the priests, didn't want to rock the boat. And Melody. She was a nut.

"I'm coming down," Freddie said, "I know I'm intruding, but we have to talk." He sat next to her, arranged a sweater over her shoulders.

She shivered, pulled the sweater tight across her chest as the furnace kicked in. "I saw the pills. I should have been there for you."

"I have been sick," he said. "Almost died. Jeff saved me."

She rested her hand on his bony knee.

The floor above them creaked.

"Sorry to drop all this on you," he said. "I'm better. Just need to gain some weight. It's not a death sentence like it used to be."

The floor above them creaked again.

"Jeff is pacing," Freddie said. "He's a wreck, wants to show you something. Let's go upstairs."

"I'll be up in a bit," Marge said. She'd always suspected that Freddie was gay, but didn't know how to deal with it. She'd even made an appointment to talk to Father Cramer, but had canceled at the last minute, knowing what he would say. When Freddie moved to San Diego, she was relieved—relieved to see her son move two thousand miles away, something she hadn't admitted to herself until right now. He could have died. What kind of a mother was she? She sat until her toes were cold and her back aching. Maybe she should kill herself. She'd abandoned her first child, had been forced to give her up for adoption, failed Freddie. Who knew what she did to Melody to make her the way she is, and Irene didn't even know her most days. What difference did it make. Above her, the floor creaked again.

"Are you coming up?" Freddie called down to her.

"In a minute." Somehow she managed to drag her body up the stairs.

Jeff sat at the piano and gestured for her to sit next to him. "I'm going to teach you how to play Chopsticks," he said.

"Well, why not?" she said. "It's certainly been a day." She took a sip of the wine Freddie handed her, happy that they hadn't offered her the pipe, set it on top of the piano and sat down next to Jeff. She remembered Irene and her friend Betty playing Chopsticks over and over until her mother would tell them to go outside.

"Start here," Jeff said and put her fingers on F and G. "Okay. One, two, three, four, five, six, one, two, three, four five, six…"

Before long she had it.

Thurs. p.m.

Irene,

A two-postcard day. I learned how to play Chopsticks and had a glass of wine in the middle of the day. I did have to take a nap before supper. I have decided that I will be there for you, and for Freddie. He may not need me, but I will be there, for now. I will be there.

Marge

About the Author

Inspired by the stories of Alice Munro, Carol Wobig started writing when she retired from making sauce in a pizza factory. Her award-winning work has appeared in *Rosebud* and other literary journals, and her monologues have been performed in community theater. Learn more at carolwobig.com.

Made in the USA
Middletown, DE
19 March 2018